AND THE COCK CREW

And the Cock Crew

FIONN *Mac* COLLA

SOUVENIR PRESS

First published by William Maclellan, Glasgow, in 1945
Published by John S. Burns & Sons, Glasgow, in 1962

This edition Copyright © 1977 by Souvenir Press and Mary
MacDonald and published 1977 by Souvenir (Educational &
Academic) Ltd., 43 Great Russell Street, London WC1B 3PA and
simultaneously in Canada by Methuen Publications, Agincourt,
Ontario

Reprinted 1983

*The publisher acknowledges the financial assistance of The Scottish Arts
Council in the production of this volume*

ISBN 0 285 62290 0 paperback

Printed in Great Britain by
Photobooks (Bristol) Ltd.

" And the Lord said: Simon, Simon, behold Satan hath desired to have you, that he may sift you as wheat . . .

" Peter said: Lord, I am ready to go with thee, both into prison and to death.

" And He said: I say to thee, Peter, the cock shall not crow this day till thou thrice deniest that thou knowest me."

ST. LUKE XXII.

CHAPTER ONE

Two men emerged through the bottle-neck of a glen mouth into a thin and wintry dawn. A wind out of the north-east narrow and bone-seeking and with an icy tooth blew at once into their faces so that they halted together to muffle themselves more closely in their plaids.

To north and south in the thinning dusk the nearer hills were momently approaching their height and form; but a dense and obscure greyness still enveloped the more distant. Below, the breadth of the Machair could already be seen dimly, the plain coastal region with fields and trees and farmhouses. And beyond— heavy and flat and leaden dull, its farthest edges stretching away under the east, and in places with a leaden sheen—the Eastern Sea.

The two figures stood high on the hill track, muffled against the keen and thrusting wind. One of them—he appeared to be the older man—made a low exclamation, catching at the end of his plaid as it was whipped from his shoulder.

" This is cold," he said.

They were silent a short while, their eyes looking about at the world rising through the cold light of daybreak.

" How is your foot now? " said the taller without looking round, in a voice somewhat indistinct by reason of the plaid edge protecting his mouth.

" It is painful enough."

The other looked about him. " We can rest over there till they reach here."

There was a cairn of stones below the track. They stepped through the dry and brittle heather and sat down in its lee.

The taller man walked with a supple stride; a groan escaped the other as he lowered himself slowly, and leaning back against the stones he made a sighing noise of relief and satisfaction.

They remained silent and without moving while the light grew and behind the blunt hill that faced them rose up the dim shape of another, and higher. Then the older man made a noise in his throat, straightened himself stiffly and bent forward. Taking hold of his leg by the ankle he raised the foot and propped it on a stone. He began pressing the ankle with the palms of his hands and groaning and exclaiming to himself in a low voice. "My grief, the pain! This is dreadful!"

"Great are your troubles, poor man," said the other, whose eyes were fixed gravely on the grey confusion where sky and hills mingled together, still undefined: and he added reflectively, " And maybe you are only at the start of them."

The other with gingerly care propped his foot more comfortably, and sitting up leant his back against the stones.

" I'm much afraid of it, my friend. Much afraid. I'll confess to you I'm uneasy, and that there's something I don't understand about things nowadays. At one time everything was plain enough. A man had only to do what was right; to labour for daily bread for himself and them that depended on him, to help another that was in need, to live at home and at peace with his neighbours. But now it seems there's something else as well. A man's duty is not fulfilled when he fears God and attends quietly to what concerns him. Something else has come among us, something from altogether outside our way and our life, and a man has to take account of it although he doesn't even understand it or know what it wants from him. Only the Black Foreigner yonder knows it, for he belongs to it, with his constant vexations. Nowadays a man has to honour God and the Factor." He slowly drew in and expelled a breath. "No indeed, it's not a simple matter to understand things nowadays. To-day's business, for instance. What do you suppose is the reason for it? What is your opinion? "

" I know as much about that as yourself, worthy man."

The older man had turned his face toward his companion. When he saw that he was to add nothing to his reply but kept his eyes fixed with a kind of sombre gravity on the hills, he continued. "Then you know nothing whatever. Neither does any one of us. Among ourselves at home nothing else has been spoken about since the minister interpreted to us the paper from the Black Foreigner. And still we know no more than that man and woman and child are summoned this day to Dùn Eachainn. Yesterday a number of us were in a house discussing the question, and every man with his own answer. Some put forward one reason and some another. But most of all we were discussing the minister, Maighstir Tormod, who is telling us that because of our sins a great and terrible calamity will fall on us, the beginning of beginnings of God's judgment because we have resisted His will; and that this is that beginning. At the end an old white-bearded cripple man from another part,—Fearchar, they were calling him; some bard or other, I believe—got up from the corner where he had been sitting all the time without saying a word, and stepped towards the door. It seems simple enough to me, says he. It means the Law has reached the glens. Therefore look well to yourselves. And he gave his bonnet a scrug and went out."

As he said this something caused him to raise his eyes. A little group had emerged from the glen mouth and were standing on the track above them: an old man was leaning on a staff and with one hand keeping the plaid to his throat; a young man was in the act of stooping to let a child climb on his back. They moved off slowly. A man appeared leading a horse on which a woman sat holding an infant in her arms. Without pausing they followed the others. After them came a large number of people drawn out in long irregular procession; men and women of all ages, and children; on foot and on horseback, and some in carts that tilted about; all moving on at the pace of the weakest and most infirm. As each group came out through the narrow opening the cold light of daybreak fell over them and their faces lit with a ghostly paleness. The bitter north-east wind met them suddenly, icy, penetrating, making the old and thin-blooded wince and shiver. Some of the youngest ones raised a shrill crying.

A little later all had emerged from the narrow glen mouth and were making their way down a sloping track towards the level ground. No one spoke. Many faces were set and grim, others looked weary or apprehensive. The only sounds were the sound of feet, the occasional clink of a horseshoe striking rock, here and there the creaking of wheels, harness jingling; and some of the children could not stop their sobbing and wailing. Now and then the bitter wind rose to a thin shrilling. At one point some message seemed to pass without speech through the company. As if obeying a common impulse all turned their heads and looked down to the left. It was already clear day, wintry and hard, and below them, coming from farther north, another long procession was clearly to be seen winding its way across the plain. Thereafter as they went forward many would turn their eyes and silently look as with the curiosity of distance at the other company crawling across the Machair.

Something had happened. Those that were following suddenly found their advance blocked by those in front and became aware that the leaders had halted. They drew up, and in their turn halted those that came behind. The whole line came to a standstill closely massed together. A few old people weary beyond interest at once seized the opportunity to drop out and rest themselves. The majority remained crowded on the track, turning their heads, unable to understand why they had halted. Voices broke out; What is it? Why have we stopped? Gradually all heads began to turn of one accord in the same direction. The voices ceased. Every eye became fixed with a mute enquiry and apprehension on a point in the middle distance, a little to the left. Miles away across the Machair it was possible to make out yet another band of people. But there was something about this company which even at that distance caught and held the eye. Something unusual. It was advancing directly from the south, not from the hill country, and approaching Dùn Eachainn. It was not strung out and irregular like the groups of people from the hills but had a definite and clearly a deliberate formation. First was a dense body on foot, then a gap in which there were horses drawing some kind of carriages or carts, then a body in close order, more horses, finally another body on foot. The whole company moved with a strange regular motion, rhythmic and unbroken, strange yet strangely familiar and in some obscure way disquieting.

An excitement ran through the people on the hillside; they drew together and their eyes stared. They had understood. Those on the plain *were marching!* From time to time the hidden sun had been shooting down long shafts of light; pale feet that the moving clouds made run in burnished brass along the dark surface of the sea. One of these mounted the shore and came at great speed in a transverse course across the plain. It passed over the marching column and a quick gasp went up from the staring people. For a single second a flash had leapt out and run like the lightning down the distant line. *Arms!* The people broke into panic. They swayed about, not knowing where to turn, pushing this way and that. On all sides, alarmed voices were heard crying, " The red soldiers! We are to be murdered! We are lost! " Women drew their plaids over their faces and began keening in high wailing voices, swaying to and fro. And everywhere, shouted fearfully or whispered in tones of terror, " The soldiers! The red soldiers! " The whole company began pressing backwards and recoiling up the track.

They were stopped by a tall gaunt figure in the rear. The minister had from the start been riding last of all so that any that fell out or thought to return found him there to turn them and urge them on. He now threw out his long arms and waved them up and down, as one heads off a straying flock. " On! On! " he shouted in a hollow loud voice. " What would you do, O people? Would you resist God's judgment? Submit! Submit! Submit! before a worse thing befall you! "

Confronted with the excited and gesticulating figure, the foremost hesitated and drew back, throwing the others into greater confusion. The minister advanced upon them, waving his arms. " The wrath of God is on you! " he shouted. " Submit! Submit! "

The men looked about in confusion and fear. The women keened and wailed in terror. A few ran forward and threw themselves before him, clutching his stirrups, his thin knees. " Have mercy, Maighstir Tormod! You are our safety, our protection! Save us! Pity us, Maighstir Tormod! "

The minister shook them off.

" On! On! It is the will of God! . . ."

2

It was past noon. The sun had not appeared and against the level hardness of stone-grey sky the roofs and turrets of Dùn Eachainn were knife-edged. The scene was everywhere an equal grey, except where the tunics of the soldiers made a line of vivid scarlet along the castle front. There was a seeking cold. Before long it would snow.

" '. . . and did pursue the said Frederick Reid and threaten him and put him in a state of bodily fear . . .' "

The small legal personage interrupted his reading every moment to cast a nervous, apprehensive glance at the crowd of people in front of him, and now and then he reassured himself by a quick look behind to measure the distance between him and the military. It seemed he supposed the people capable of making a sudden furious rush and in spite of the bayonets of the soldiers and the loaded cannon trained on them at little more than forty paces, pursuing him and threatening him and putting him in a state of even greater bodily fear.

For their part the people understood nothing of what was going on. To the number of over two thousand they stood crowded together on the open space before Dùn Eachainn— venerable, white-bearded men, aged women, little children, the middle-aged, the youthful—a whole population. They huddled together in the bitter wind, silent, awed and defenceless. Many of the men had taken off their bonnets and stood uncovered. Of the indictment being read out against them as it was in English they understood nothing. They supposed only that they had been brought there to be murdered. They saw their executioners, the English soldiery of legendary frightfulness. They had no protector. They merely waited for the massacre to begin. Their eyes, charged with dismay and horror, some with a kind of anguished hope, a few full of hate and anger, looked at the nervous little man standing in front of the guns reading a document in a thin excited voice; at the Black Foreigner beside him, smiling; at the line of red soldiers; at the two ministers. They looked at each in turn, but with scarce hope in any. They were told they had incurred the incomprehensible wrath of the Almighty, and many believed that God had abandoned them.

His misgivings would hardly permit the small legal personage to finish the reading, and indeed he was still speaking the last few words when he skipped down from the little knoll and scuttled behind the military, where he incontinent took snuff. The Factor, whom they called the Black Foreigner, bared his white teeth in a still wider grin. From the beginning he had smiled; but not with amusement. When he saw so many of the people together, by his command and almost at his mercy, he was filled with rage. But it was their defencelessness above all that inflamed him. He could not look at them huddled together, deserted and pitiful, without being exasperated to a lust of cruel hate. He raged inwardly against the limits of his power and could hardly restrain the impulse to loose all control and throwing away the last pretences of legality call out on the military to fire. His smile was calm and cold.

He left his position and strode directly towards the people.

Seeing the broad and burly figure bearing down on them, clothed with the representative mystery of a distant impersonal power to which they had no access and from which they knew of no appeal, they stiffened, expecting the blow. It is coming, they thought. *Now* it is to happen.

A similar anticipation seemed to affect the military. Their stout, purple-faced officer was standing a few paces in advance of the line, and by the stiff air of consequence he had maintained from the beginning at the cost of considerable personal strain, it could be seen he thought highly enough of his importance to the situation. He stood in a rigid military attitude, his heels together. His toes unfortunately pointed rather far apart. His legs too, as if from supporting so much corpulence, bent a little inwards so that his plump knees rested one against the other. He bore himself with heavy dignity, looking straight before him into space, but with so fixed impersonal a gaze as made it doubtful whether in fact he was really seeing anything. Sometimes however as if becoming aware of the reader's voice he glanced aside at him. He would thereupon turn his eyes which were rather small towards the cowed and dispirited people; his too tightly stretched tunic expanded dangerously, his thick neck swelled in his collar, and he bent on them a stern, reproving glance, as if with a look to curb their rebellious spirit and acquaint them with the salutary fact that in him they had to deal with one who knew no fear nor relenting in the exercise of duty.

Seeing the Factor now striding away with a purposeful air in the direction of the people he wheeled round towards his men. His neck thickened. He barked an order. All became rigid at their posts, every man looking straight before him with an expressionless face. He cast up and down the line a severe and threatening look, and having satisfied himself that all, muskets and cannon, were ready for instant action, faced again to the front. He assumed a fierce and warlike expression and directed upon the people a most threatening scowl, swelling inside his straining tunic, puffing up his purplish cheeks and blowing out his moustaches with martial ardour. It was clear that if the people did break out in rebellion the military at least were ready to face the conflict without flinching.

The two ministers had begun by standing a little in front of their flocks. The proceedings had hardly opened however before the tall gaunt minister began to gloom about him as if he were uneasy. The other minister was small and round with plump cheeks like a ripe apple. But although the broad smile never left his rosy face he too appeared to suffer from some inquietude. He kept nervously moving his feet, and his eyes which seemed to have a twinkling expression never rested. Before long it might have seemed the ministers were not so near the people. A little later there was no doubt about it; they had moved by imperceptible degrees some distance away. In the end they were some twenty paces distant and almost half-way to the military.

When the Black Foreigner advanced the tall minister made several strides forward into his path. The small plump minister hurried with little bounding steps to arrive along with him. The Factor neither halted nor altered his course. Striding on his way he brushed against the ministers who were hastily drawing back out of his path; and gave them not so much as a look.

He halted some ten paces in front of the people.

Taking out a long paper he unrolled it and prepared as if to read. But first he raised his angry eyes under his black brows and passed them, without haste, over the faces of the people. If his intention was to glower them out of countenance he must have been gratified by what he saw. The person was not there who could afford to regard him with indifference. He had long been an object of fear to many. And by these last events, seeing themselves abandoned and supposing their plight to be beyond hope of succour, even the strong-hearted had been made dispirited and submissive. Many did not care even to meet his eye and few indeed returned him look for look.

He turned again to his paper and all waited in fear for what he would read. He said nothing. A minute passed. Still he kept silence, looking at the paper with as calm a front as if he were a man reading an indifferent matter in solitude. Another minute . . . Quite clearly he was determined that nothing should be omitted from their suffering. They were convinced the blow must fall: this was torture . . .

Suddenly, the strain snapped. Women shrieked aloud. Many men even had made startled exclamations. The children burst everywhere into a terrified screaming and wailing.

People looked into each other's faces in consternation, their eyes asking, What has happened?

It was the Factor. Having waited until the strain touched the point beyond which it was not to be borne he had suddenly lifted a ferocious face and roared out two words in a voice like a bull. And the people strained past endurance had been so startled that they cried out and did not know what he had said.

" Donal' Munro, Woodend! " He shouted the name again. " Donal' Munro! "

No reply came. His brow flushed. He roared out in the loudest and most terrifying voice, " Donal' Munro! " But although he assumed a ferocious aspect, glaring here and there among the faces, he met only looks of perplexity, or fear, or blank incomprehension. He thought the man was not present, and at the thought of such defiance grew crimson.

" If Donal' Munro is no' here . . . ! "

Words failed him for anger. He raised his fist. It looked as if he would have leapt upon the people.

The two ministers had been standing a short distance away. After consulting together a moment they came forward and said something to the Factor who knitted his brows at the interruption but nevertheless turned aside to hear their say. Both spoke to him a little, eagerly, as if convincing him. Listening to them he made angry impatient movements, but in the end seemed to agree to something. The plump, smiling minister approached the people.

" Is Domhnall Mac-an-Rothaich here? " he called out in the Gaelic language. " Domhnall Meadhonach, from Ceann-na-Coille! "

At once all the heads began turning. " Domhnall Meadhonach Mac-an-Rothaich "—the name went from mouth to mouth.

Near the far end of the line a man appeared in front of the others but made no attempt to approach the minister. He seemed to be trying to get back into the crowd, while the others pushed him forward, encouraging him.

" Come here, Domhnall," called out the plump minister, still smiling.

The man began to walk along the front of the line, but slowly and with a hesitating step. Now and then he stopped and made as if to retreat. He seemed to be moving his head about with a kind of rolling motion. Indeed there was something a little peculiar about his movements and his whole appearance. As he came on he was smiling.

Having reached the place where the minister was standing he came to a halt and took off his bonnet. He was a middle-sized and middle-aged man, almost completely bald, and bare-faced except for a few long hairs growing out of his chin. His face fell serious all at once. The eyes he turned on the minister had a childishly grave enquiring expression.

The small plump minister had assumed a solemn, important aspect; when he stopped smiling it was seen that the smile was no more than a mannerism and his eyes were not merry at all.

" Are you Domhnall Meadhonach?" says he, importantly.

The man seemed surprised. He raised his arm and drew his sleeve along his mouth. He looked at the people. He looked all round him. Finally he looked back at the minister and broke into a grin.

The minister was annoyed. " Are you Domhnall from Ceann-na-Coille?" he said roughly.

The man looked at him a moment as if doubtful. " *Maighstir Iain!*" he protested in a laughing, reproachful tone. He broke into a wide grin of pure amusement, wagging his head and swaying from foot to foot.

The minister frowned and turned to the people.

" Is this Domhnall Mac-an-Rothaich from Ceann-na-Coille?" he said in a testy voice. " The man they call Domhnall Meadhonach?"

There was a silence.

" That is Domhnall, poor man," said a voice.

The minister turned again.

" Well now, Domhnall," says he in a tone suddenly condescending and friendly. "Tell me, why did you run after the gentleman like yon and frighten him?"

The man looked perplexed again. He regarded the minister a little and a hurt expression began to come into his eyes. He shook his head slowly from side to side. "I don't know what . . ." he said in a low voice. "I'm not understanding you, Minister."

"Now, now, Domhnall, surely you heard what the gentleman was reading out of the big paper?"

The man seemed distressed, shaking his head doubtfully. He spoke slowly, in a low voice.

"I could hardly say with truth that I did, Minister. I heard indeed a certain noise of speaking in the English language, and it seemed to me that the Factor and the fat gentleman yonder in the red coat were in a rage . . ."

"Come, come, Domhnall!" the minister interrupted with a great show of sudden indignation. "Is that a way to speak?"

Domhnall now looked a little frightened. "What is my fault, Maighstir Iain? What have I done?"

"You lack respect, Domhnall. You said 'noise'; I heard you. *Noise,* indeed! Is that a word to use?" The minister's face was red. He was sticking his head forward and nodding it at the man, browbeating him. "I'm warning you, you are in great danger just now, Domhnall, and if you want to escape without a bad punishment you must tell the truth and be respectful. 'Noise' is an impudent word and not for using when you are speaking about the gentlemen's language."

"On my word I meant no offence, Minister." Domhnall saw by his red face that the minister was getting angrier. He became thoroughly frightened. His voice was submissive, almost tearful. "I have no doubt at all that it is a very, very fine language the English, a very noble language, Maighstir Iain. And truly it is a gentleman's language, too, if gentlemen speak it. But as I have not a word of it in my head I am so unfortunate that to me it is only a noise, Maighstir Iain."

"Be you very careful! Be you very careful!" The minister

was apparently angrier than ever. " This is a day for showing respect! "

" On my word and on my soul I meant no offence, Minister." The submissive voice sounded now more hurt than apologetic. The poor man had his pride too.

The minister gave him barely time to finish. " Be you careful, Domhnall Meadhonach! " he said, shouting now, and very unfortunately, whether by accident or on purpose, emphasising the nickname, *Middling* Donald. " It is time you were learning to respect your betters! You have been very wicked, you and the people here. The King himself has heard of it yonder in England. You're the greatest trouble the King has; I'm black affronted with you. He has had to send up his soldiers yonder to keep you in order, you're so bad. But even now, you don't show respect. ' The fat man in a red coat '— yon's respect for you. *Fat!* And he the King's officer himself! "

The man was watching the minister with grave eyes. A change had been coming over his face. At this point he suddenly threw up both his arms. " *Thin!* Minister! " he shrieked in a frenzied voice, his face livid and distorted. " *Thin! thin!* So thin . . . ! I never saw . . . ! " The foam came on his lips. His jaw moved up and down. He stared at the minister with a kind of astonishment, one arm arrested stiffly above his head.

The minister had drawn back with a horrified look, lifting up his hands. He turned to his companions.

" A fery tainsherous maan, Maister Byars," he said to the Factor.

" I thocht it," said the Factor with unconcealed satisfaction, at once stepping forward. " Stand you ower there, my man," he said grimly to Domhnall Meadhonach, pointing with his hand to a spot a little apart.

His sudden outburst had subsided as quickly as it arose; Domhnall looked now from one to the other with eyes full of childish contrition. As none took notice of him he turned away with a dejected air and went and stood on the spot indicated by the Factor's pointing hand.

He was not to be alone. Having consulted the Factor's

paper the plump minister called out three names at once. Three men made their way through the crowd and came and stood before him. He was to repeat his way of acting with Domhnall Meadhonach. He first asked their names. Then he drove straight to the point and demanded without further preliminary what excuse they had to make for having threatened the strange gentleman with violence, pursued him, and put him in bodily fear. All protested they had done nothing and did not understand the question. As before, he flew into a rage and began to browbeat them and take them up on their replies. But the Factor had been showing signs of impatience. All the talking back and fore in a language he did not understand exasperated him. He could not remain quietly in the background while the minister had his say with the unresisting people. He came forward and pushed past the minister. " Ower there! " he said to the three men. " Ower there wi' ye! " He smiled faintly watching them go bewildered towards Domhnall Meadhonach. Then he turned, frowning, and called out another name. The small plump minister looked hurt. He retired a step, pouting.

But at this point something very unexpected occurred. Some commotion got up right in the middle of the people. Voices were heard, and one of them unmistakably raised in anger. Every head turned, necks were craned. A kind of swirling movement was going on there and this swirl began to travel forward through the crowd. There could be no doubt about it, an angry voice was making its way to the front!

The two ministers looked at each other in consternation when the figure appeared in front of the line. The Factor gave a half-startled " *Ah!*"—and clapped his mouth shut.

It was a strong-looking reddish man, wearing his bonnet. He was about the middle size, but looked both larger and redder because he was buzzing with rage.

The Factor strode rapidly forward, but the angry man was quicker than he and mounted the little knoll and looked down at him. The Factor halted, his face dark. But he mastered himself before he spoke.

" Ah, Meenister! so ye *are* here! I was juist wonderin'

what had come ower ye." His tone was bantering, his smile twisted with anger. "What's the meanin' o' this?" he burst out.

The people were in agitation, turning to each other. Exclamations were heard, "Maighstir Sachairi! Maighstir Sachairi!" The blaeberry-complexioned officer had noticed the diversion. He scowled, expanded inside his tunic, and began to cast warlike glances. The face of the little legal personage appeared for a moment among the soldiers, and was hastily withdrawn.

The man standing on the knoll looked the Factor straight in the eye. His whole aspect and bearing expressed a powerful indignation; but it was an anger perfectly in control.

"I *am* here, Maister Byars," he said. "Ye need wonder no longer. As for the reason o' 't—I am come for no purpose at all but to tell ye." He spoke his Scots-English with a strong Gaelic flavour, aspirated and hissing at the s's.

"Ye're meddlin' wi' what's nae business o' yours, Meenister! It's a serious maitter to oppose the Law, mind ye!"

"*I* am not opposing the Law, Maister Byars."

"Ye are that! Ye're a great man wi' theology, Maister Wiseman, and I hear ye're a king, nae less, in your ain parish; but I'm warnin' ye to gang canny wi' the Law."

"I am *not* opposing the Law, Maister Byars. And I will say this—let the Law judge whether you or me is most outside the Law in our actions this day! I am not a judge of sic matters, but I have a strong suspeecion that much of this day's work is without the forms of Law."

"That's an accusation!" cried the Factor, raging.

"Weel if it is, Maister Byars, I will not insist on it. The Law as you say is a kittle business. But I will tak' better ground and tell ye it was agin justice. Ye were good enough to notice I wasna beside my brethren yonder." (His glance at the two ministers was tinged with disfavour.) "And I will now tell ye my reason. I wasna yonder, Maister Byars, because I had doubts about this business frae the start; and I wouldna be seeming to approve the affair afore my doubts were putten at rest. I preferred to bide where ye might expect one of my calling to bide in a time of trouble " (he glanced again at the ministers)—" among his people. And if I misliked the affair afore, I like it less now. I would think shame to be in your shoon, Maister Byars. Ye have brought thegether decent well-doing fowk and feared them o' their lives with sodgers and cannons. And what is more ye have taken poor men that didna understand a word ye said and couldna resist ye and roared and glowered at them like dirt and put them in mortal fear—and worst of all one o' them as ye could easy see a poor body without his share of sense."

" Sense enough, Meenister! " the Factor interrupted, furious and barely controlling himself. " Sense enough to be a veecious lawbreakin' deevil. And I would have ye ken, sir, that puir bodies here or puir bodies there thae men foregathered a fortnicht syne with intent to commit a breach o' the peace, being weel kent for rebellious and ill-affected subjects. And we have the man that was putten in fear by them, running thegether and threatening and jabbering in the Gaelic."

" As for that last, Maister Byars, I am myself a Scotchman and speak the Gaelic language, though I ken ye well for its enemy. But I'm no aware that the Law permits ye to seize the persons of them that are guilty of not jabbering in the English. Just at the present moment, Factor, it isna a criminal offence to speak the Gaelic, and if it please ye we will no' discuss it. The other is the important thing, and we will speak about *that*. I'm no althegether ignorant of this matter myself, and I believe indeed I can now tell ye the right way of it."

He paused, drew himself up and fixed his eye on the Factor as if daring him to interrupt. The end of his plaid, blowing out behind him, quivered and leapt in the wind as though inspired with his own indignation. The Factor, compelled by their respective positions to look upwards, returned him a glare full of impotent fury. The paper he had been consulting was crushed up in one of his clenched fists . . .

About a fortnight before, some of the men of those parts

had foregathered in the course of their normal business. It happened that one of them had been looking about him, and there his eye fell on a stranger. The stranger was sitting on horseback, shading his eyes with his hand and looking attentively first this way and then that. The first man drew the attention of his companions. " Yon stranger will have lost himself," he said. They watched. The stranger moved to another position, looking about him. Sometimes in an effort to see better he crouched and lowered his head, and sometimes he raised himself and stretched his neck. He had not observed the men as yet. " He is lost, surely," said another. A third said, " We will put him on his road." They approached, and one of them asked the man where he wished to go. But at the first word he turned round on them a startled face. His mouth fell open and he remained staring at them, speechless with fright. The men were amused at his frightened look and the start he had given, and a few of them asked again, laughingly, if he had lost his way and where he wished to go. To their amazement he remained as if petrified, with a look of terror. They could make nothing of this. Some of them thought he might be deaf. One said in a shouting voice, making the words with his mouth, " Are—you—*lost?*" For answer the man startled them by suddenly putting spurs to his horse. Once when he was already at a distance he turned his face over his shoulder and shouted something in an unknown tongue and made a flourish with his arm in the air. Then his horse's tail disappeared over a ridge of rising ground . . .

" And that, Maister Byars, is what happened yonder. That's the *true* story."

" *No!*" The Factor lifted his fist and shook it in emphasis above his head. " No! Maister Zachary! There's mair nor that! Ye've stopped ower shune! "

Maighstir Sachairi pounced on him.

" Ye're right, Factor! There *is* mair! What for do ye think the man Reid would be that easy flegged? How would he be thinking a pickle harmless bodies meant him ill, think ye? I will tell ye, Maister Byars. I will tell ye what was flegging

the man Reid. It was the man Reid's conscience. It wasna
the men that meant ill to *him!* No: but he meant ill to *them.*
That was what feared him. And he kenned forbye that if they
had jaloused what was in his mind yonder they would have
had good cause to do him a mischeef. What *was* in his mind,
Maister Byars, think ye? I think I ken; and I'm much mistaken if you dinna. The man Reid is a sheep man; no' the
first, more's the peety, that has come this road seeking siller
to himself and no good at all to the lave o' us. At the very
minute the decent men went in-ower to do him a service,
thinking he was a stranger gotten out of his road—at that
very meenute the man Reid was reckoning in his head what
worth their places would be to him if he could but turn them
out into the world and beggar them. With sic thoughts in his
head it was like a clap of conscience to find them at his
elbock. It is no wonder to me the man couldna bide and
took his feet for it. If he was pursued it was by his conscience
jabbering at him, and the fear he was in wasna bodily. That's
my opeenion for ye, Maister Byars, and I would like to ken
what ye could put to it and better it! "

   The blood of anger was in the Factor's face; he bit his lip.

   " Ye're speaking your mind, Maister Zachary! "

   " I will speak it out, Maister Byars. If the men yonder were
guilty of what ye lay to their charge—and I believe they are
eennocent—it would aye be a somewhat treevial offence and
could have been dealt wi' by a two-three officers o' the peace.
Instead of that ye set a day and time and order and command the population of a haill neighbourhood to appear afore
ye, showing conseederation neither to auld men nor bairns,
nor even eediots. Forbye that ye turn Balnambó intil a
poother-magazine. Ye send for cannons and regiments of
sodgers and get ready for a ceevil war. Ye're no' a fule,
Maister Byars. Ye dinna do sic things without ye have your
reasons. Ye maun admit this is a byordinar' way o' doing,
and ye canna wonder if it starts the question what would be
your reason for seeking to put this haill countryside in terror
o' their lives.

   " As it happens the question is no' ill to answer. It is no

secret to myself and my brethren yonder that some time syne
ye took it on yourself to decide that this neighbourhood
would suit ye better if its population had fower feet instead
of two. And to that ye have the knowledge and consent of
your maister yonder in England. What! Maister Byars! ye
would deny it? Ye needna fash; I have it on the word no less
of my brethren yonder, who had it from yourself, that ye
have at this very meenute notices-to-quit all ready to be
served on every household among the people there. Right
weel ye ken what that will mean for them, Factor. A sentence
of exile and beggary. And for some of them daith even. And
because the intentions of your heart are black, black agin
them ye're feared o' them that they'll oppose ye and turn on
ye. So ye are taking the chance to fear them out of their lives
aforehand with your cannons and your English sodgers in the
hope that come the day they will no' resist ye. My brethren
yonder profess to see in this the avenging hand of God, and
I am told they have been preparing their people to expect a
seengular judgment. It is no' my place to be putting my
brethren right, and I will say therefore that it *may* be the
judgment of God. But I will say further and on the other
hand that it may *not*. And if so be it is no' the judgment of
God, Maister Byars, then it can be nothing more nor the
oppressions of men. I am saying in that case—are ye hearing?
—it is just the oppressions of men!

" Maister Byars! I will ask ye to cast your e'e on the
people there. I ken them, as do ye, for as peaceable and
well-doing as any within this kingdom. The great part of
them have passed their lives respected and independent.
Many have been accustomed to enjoy a-plenty of this world's
goods, and they have spent of their abundance in charity to
the poor and hospitality to the stranger. There was never a
door of one of them but was aye open to any that passed by,
and many's the time that man has been yourself. They are a
people upright, peaceable, temperate in their ways and
righteous with their neighbours to a most seengular degree in
our times and generation. Maister Byars! the Providence of
God has seen fit to put this people in your power: and how

have ye used your power! Sparing neither the grey head nor the bairn at the knee, ye have made all to rise out of their beds afore daybreak this bitter day and make their different ways with doubts and sore misgivings. Ye have feared them to death the space of three mortal hours and never took peety on their agony. And ye bear it in your heart to make them paupers and houseless wanderers and give their hearthstanes to four-footed beasts.

"Maister Byars! there is one God abune us. As He has given, so He can take away, and blessed be His Name. If He will visit His wrath on us, there is none that can withstand Him. But He has bestowed a flock into my keeping. And if wolves break through the fold—I am Sachairi Wiseman, the servant of Jesus Christ, not of men. He has given into my care the orphan and the defenceless. In the day of bloody men *I* will be their protector!"

The minister stopped speaking, holding a hand above his head. The two looked straight into each other's eyes: and both understood the look . . . *Battle was joined!*

The Factor turned his broad back and strode from the field.

Maighstir Sachairi turned towards the people. They had understood from his aspect and the tones of his voice that he was speaking in their cause. All fixed their eyes on him with an anxious question, but now daring to hope. He addressed them in their own language.

"You have nothing more to fear. Yon soldiers have no power to hurt you. Disperse quietly and return at once to your homes. Let this day be for a warning to you to trust God and fear Him, Who alone is able to defend you. And see that you comport yourselves prudently and without offence towards them that are over you, so that they may be without excuse. Go now!"

Maighstir Sachairi remained watching the people streaming away. His serious and thoughtful look deepened away from the scene before him into an absorbed gravity . . .

Hearing the voice behind him, he wheeled round, alert.

During the minister's passage with the Factor the small legal personage had several times run out from behind the military as if with a purpose, and at once retreated again to safety. This time his courage held; he had reached his former standing place and having produced another document, was excitedly reading from it.

Maighstir Sachairi raised his eyebrows and looked at him a little, listening. Then with a little shrug of indifference he turned his back. The space before him had emptied with wonderful rapidity; the remainder of the people were now hurrying from the scene. His eye fell on Domhnall Mead-honach and his three companions still standing, irresolutely, looking at him. " Go now," he said. " You too. For the present you are safe."

The legal person continued to read at the pitch of his thin voice:

" Our Sovereign Lord the King chargeth and commandeth all persons being assembled immediately to disperse them-selves and peaceably to depart to their habitations or to their lawful business upon the pains contained in the Act made in the first year of King George for preventing tumults and riotous assemblies. *God Save the King!"*

He raised his eyes. There was nobody in sight.

The snow had come on at last.

CHAPTER TWO

M AIGHSTIR SACHAIRI was shocked and dismayed. In all his life he had never stumbled upon so scandalous an instance, nor had so unpleasingly thrust before him the depravity of hearts.

Sin! When he came to Gleann Luachrach he had found plenty of it. At that time men were possessed by a spirit of impious levity, wholly given to worldliness and Satan's service. There was nothing greater with them at that time than to excel in the popular forms of vanity and he was most esteemed whose arms most lustily swung the hammer, whose foot was swiftest in the race, or fingers nimblest on the chanter, whose voice was sweetest in singing of old wars and carnal love and profanity, whose wit most often overwhelmed the other in the louder laughter. It was nothing for the pipes to make their appearance even at the Sacraments, so that the worship of God was scarcely done before the young people were over the wall and busy dancing, the while their elders gossiped and jested shamelessly among the graves and (as was likely) some old cailleach, namely for quickness of tongue, sat on a tombstone and amid the immoderate unseemly mirth of admiring acquaintance held her court and engaged all comers. He had thought in those days that contempt of Godliness could go no farther.

He was the less prepared for *this*. Taking him at unawares it had overthrown his customary balance and cast his mind into a state in which a sense of outrage contended with simple bewilderment. *Mairi!* Mairi-daughter-of-Eoghann-Gasda! The very *last* person! . . .

Maighstir Sachairi looked again at the young woman sitting on a low stool at the other side of the fire. The light from the window behind him fell on her face, on the smooth clear brow and downcast eyelids, the features composed with seemly modesty. She held her hands clasped together demurely in her lap, patiently waiting for what it pleased him to do or say. The very type of pure and modest womanhood, he thought. He could not believe it of her.

" *Mairi!*" He said the name aloud, as if the sound of his familiar voice might have imposed on things their common aspect and recalled the wonted proportions that had suddenly deserted them. He was trying to recover himself and to know what it was his proper part to say or do in a situation so unprecedented, so far beyond anything he might have thought or imagined, that it had taken out of his hands every weapon whose use he knew.

" Then you refuse to tell his name?"

She neither moved nor raised her eyes.

" I have answered that already, Maighstir Sachairi."

Her tone was soft and submissive, but perfectly calm, perfectly firm. His own confusion increased the more; he was again without words. His eyes with a hurt and troubled expression in their depths returned to their wandering in an unseeing manner from object to object in the room. The silence was renewed, and in it there began to be heard the breathing noise from where the crone, decrepit and scarcely living, lay propped up in the shadows of the bed. A turf of peat collapsed in the fire and a small crackling followed the faint thud of its falling. Maighstir Sachairi became aware that the white object in front of his eyes was some living thing. He looked. A hen that had come in unobserved was sticking its neck out from under the counterpane of the bed. With its head held on one side the creature was regarding him inquisitively. It gave a cluck and throwing its head on the other side regarded him with the other eye. It withdrew its neck and now only its yellow feet were visible. One was drawn up and disappeared, to reappear a little in advance of the other. The hen began to strut slowly along behind the counterpane, clucking at each step. Maighstir Sachairi allowed his thoughtful, troubled gaze to follow the strutting feet.

For some reason at that moment what had been incomprehensible became clear. He understood from what reversal of their positions his confusion arose. In the presence of one who was bound to stand in virtue of his office for a judge and an accuser, whether he used her gently or with the angers of the Law, a fallen woman was bound to be shamefaced. But he had encountered here the very aspect of purity and innocence, the serene front of virtue conscious of itself. And it was *he* who turned aside and whose words faltered. He should have lashed her guilt with whips—and he sat before her in a kind of helplessness, with confusion of face. He understood that the prisoner had disarmed the judge, and the accuser was somehow become a suppliant. But he did not understand whence she derived the power to force on him such a reversal of his part, and herself to maintain an aspect so contrary to what befitted her. She was a woman fallen from the household of faith and virtue—*foul thought!* the daughter of Eoghann Gasda become a haunter of ditches! Her guilt was on her. She was a corrupt thing, a very stench of wantonness, and deserved not mercy but judgment, not pity but a curse.

" It's on myself the two days have come," he said, but in spite of him he sounded no more than reproachful, " when I see your father's daughter no better than a . . ."

He saw the flush of shame redden suddenly on her neck and brow, and faltered into confusion and silence. The word he had been about to say uttered itself in his head as he looked at her. He knew that he was blushing too and felt the skin grow hot over his cheekbones.

Whether she noticed his confusion and took pity on him it was she that broke the silence. Not looking at him but raising her eyes and fixing them on the fire she said in a low but steady voice, " You know, Maighstir Sachairi, that the Black Foreigner has sent out an order to the people of Gleann Mór, that if any man marries a wife his land will be taken away from him and his house will be pulled down and both himself and all his family will be driven out into the world and banished from the neighbourhood."

Maighstir Sachairi at once felt himself placed on surer ground. He felt she had excused herself, and thereby admitted guilt; and her innocence was therefore only an appearance. He was in the right after all. Moreover she had committed herself to a position, and a position could be attacked, whether on the grounds of reason or theology; the person committed to a position stood to be judged either under the natural or the Divine Law. These were familiar grounds. He was no longer opposed by the unknown and intangible.

"I have heard of the Factor's highhandedness," he said. "I am not approving of it. But it is not an excuse for *you*. The tyranny of rulers is never an excuse for sin in the people. We are told to practise chastity and continence, and no exception is made of times and places. The task is never easy, and it is likely that occasions will make it more difficult, but our duty remains the same. You may be able to point to a great grievance and a real oppression, Mairi, and you may say therefore that you are not wanton but a wife kept from her husband; but such things do not make your sin the less. You have sinned, and in your sin you have shamed this parish and your family and the memory of your father. When I look at you, Mairi, I can think only that the daughter of Eoghann Gasda has come to this. At the bidding of bodily affections and desires you have disdained your father's precepts and set at naught your religious upbringing. Your excuse is no excuse, for you do not get leave to sin because tyrants are tyrannical."

The young girl had dropped her eyes on hearing his tone, and sat again in the same demure attitude, but flushing a little. She said nothing. It was impossible to tell by her look what she was thinking, or whether she had understood even. Maighstir Sachairi began again to have the disquieting sense that the situation was eluding his grasp. Succeeded by silence and an inscrutable look what he said (he began to feel) had lacked something in cogency, had not been after all exactly what it was necessary to have said. He experienced the beginning of resentment at being made to feel so. The situation was in reality perfectly clear and simple, he told himself, fearing to be put at a loss again. A minister, appointed for the rebuke of evildoers—he repeated it to himself—and a woman, brought up to know the Law and the forms of Godliness, who through inordinateness of the flesh had sinned and fallen. That was the situation. It was perfectly plain, and there was nothing mysterious about it.

So he told himself in his mind: yet he had only to look at her sitting there to experience the strange feeling that their positions were reversed, that the man of mature years and judgment was the more youthful and inexperienced, while the young woman drew a serene and confident quietness out of some more complete, or deeper, or more direct knowledge. And it was as if his view or system was suffering a silent judgment at the hands of another, less partial or superficial, which was hers.

Maighstir Sachairi felt he had to put an end to a silence which left him every moment with less ability to decide or act. It was even not reasonable to indulge the fancy that any view of the situation could be right other than what he knew to be the proper one.

" Did you hear me, Mairi?" he asked, somewhat magisterially.

" I heard, Maighstir Sachairi," she replied in her soft submissive voice. And as before she had no sooner spoken than he saw that he had been the victim of a mere fancy; she herself saw her case no other than he judged it.

" Now, Mairi," he continued, more persuasively, pressing back to the point, " you have confessed that it is a man from Gleann Mór. You did well. I will ask you again; what is his name? Without more ado, Mairi—who is he?"

The young woman had flushed scarlet at the mention of Gleann Mór. She raised her eyes in a sudden flash of anger and looked at Maighstir Sachairi. " I will not tell," she said. Turning her glance away, she made a small, bitter smile, and added meaningly, " You have made a long visit yourself, Maighstir Sachairi. I would not like to hear them slander you." Her anger died at once. She drooped her head and the tears appeared on her lashes.

Maighstir Sachairi was upset. He could not help suddenly seeing himself in a brutal part, as having bullied and driven her into tortured revolt. He got to his feet greatly embarrassed.

She got up also and accompanied him to the door. At the door she was to make him a curtsy, but because of what she carried she stumbled and put a hand to the wall to save herself from falling. Recovering herself she looked up at Maighstir Sachairi with a sudden deprecating smile.

Maighstir Sachairi had put out a solicitous hand when she stumbled. He looked at the sweet smile she gave and the tears still in her eyes, and went out with a troubled and sorrowful air.

2

The natural disposition of Maighstir Sachairi's mind was towards the inhabiting *forms* of its objects. He tended to be little conscious of parts and divisions in the things he saw. What his mind quested was totalities, what it sought to grasp in things was that which made them living and intelligible wholes—that which they were in themselves, not that of which they were composed. And this was so not only when the object was an individual—a tree, a running horse, a mountain—but also when it was formed of a number of single things—as a landscape, with hills, trees, a river, and houses.

But in Nature the forms are tossed down, thrown about, piled on one another, overlap; and it is seldom that Nature herself so disposes a number of single things that together they present to the eye a whole, which is neither their sum nor partakes of the nature of any one of them, but is another "form," a single whole, intelligible by itself. Ordinarily in Nature either an excess of parts destroys the whole, or else by the deficiency of its parts it falls short of completeness. Maighstir Sachairi was accustomed to correct the defect by his mind; constantly in whatever he was looking at—a stretch of country, a room furnished, a sky with clouds—his imagination would be at work balancing the emphasis of the parts; in his mind he would supply what was lacking, and annihilate whatever was excessive or inharmonious. And because the forms in Nature pass into each other, overlap, spread out and continue themselves in every direction, only finally completed within the total scheme of visible things, Maighstir Sachairi's habit was to imagine for himself limits within which the things at which he looked would make by themselves a harmonious whole. He did this as of necessity, because the need and nature of his mind was to seek in things the *form*, the harmonious, the complete and intelligible. And therefore he did it spontaneously, without reflection, and was not at all aware of what it was that he did.

When it was first suggested to him, tentatively, that his parish should be unpeopled, and that it would be to his advantage if, like his brethren of the ministry, he would help those that hoped to gain by it, Maighstir Sachairi had been chiefly outraged because of this disposition of his mind. The life of the glenpeople in its yearly round and seasons possessed in his eyes a shape and harmony; it appeared as a natural work of completion of unassisted Nature, on which it rested as on a base properly proportioned to it and with which it formed a single, ordered, intelligible whole. To destroy it seemed an outrage and a violation, the triumph of chaos over order. For Maighstir Sachairi had no feeling but repulsion for what was to succeed it. He could not contemplate that more crudely pastoral life of the sheep men without a deep sense of the incomplete, of frustration. It meant the forcible pushing back of completed Nature into infertility. It involved the senseless dehumanisation of a whole countryside. On every count it represented a regression, a reversal of the natural line of vital growth. But above all it was dissatisfying to him because it was a life without roots, not growing out of the soil but taking from it an illicit sustenance as it were by stealth, not needing any particular place, fixed nowhere, and therefore without vital relation to any single countryside, permanently incapable of taking root and forming with, and within, its surroundings a unity and a whole. Therefore it was a life without shape, because without natural boundaries, its edges lying in no direction or stretching away in all directions at once. The life of the glenpeople was a living whole, for it revolved about its own axis and its centre was within itself; the mind could consider it in isolation from adjacent regions and see it satisfyingly, as a unity. But given over to sheep and shepherding the life of the district would be meaningless by itself, its centre would lie outside it far away in the wool-markets and factories of the south; it would decline at once from an intelligible whole and become no more than an insignificant and not even necessary point on the circumference of a life centred elsewhere. Maighstir Sachairi's mind had revolted from such an irruption of the meaningless.

It was at such a moment that he suddenly realised all this: and it shook him. Leaving the house of Eoghann Gasda deep in his troubled mood, he had mounted his horse and ridden slowly down towards the level bottom of the glen. But his preoccupation deepened and settled on him and he was too absorbed to notice it when the animal, finding itself not urged forward and left without direction, walked more and more slowly and finally came to a standstill. For a long time he remained a conspicuous mounted figure in the centre of the valley, motionless. His head was bowed and his eyes under their thick brows looked with a distant, unseeing expression past his horse's neck at the ground. From habit he had taken out his snuffbox, but merely held it open in his hand. By a course of reflection so concentrated that he frowned deeply, he reached the point where it broke upon him what he had been doing—constantly, all those years; and why the proposal had touched him into instant, indignant opposition. Constantly, everywhere he looked, he had been seeking the satisfaction of an inner craving of his mind for harmonies, for the beauty shed by intelligibility in created forms. And as the natural man is in Sin, and the natural mind seeks what is contrary to God, *he had been sinning.* All those years. Constantly, everywhere he looked, in everything he thought or felt, he had been seeking that natural beauty and harmony that appears beauty and harmony to the unregenerate human mind, and (for the very reason that it gives satisfaction to a human mind which is in its nature sinful) cannot help but be forever and unalterably in direct opposition to God, in Whose eyes the beauty of earthly forms is by Sin turned into a loathing. He thought: I thought I was a saint of God, and I am no better than a Pagan poet or philosopher. Maighstir Sachairi's recollection went back at that moment to his youth and early manhood. To years he had spent in pursuit of vanities, occupied with fleeting fancies and imaginations of passing beauties in his earthly mind. When he remembered those years he shuddered, and began with fear to marvel at the wiles of Satan. " I thought I had renounced all that, and here for years it has been back in the very centre of my mind without my suspecting it! "

He then thought: Let me beware how I fight against God and oppose my will to His. He had detected himself in a crucial fallacy—for as he now saw clearly it could be no indication of the Divine will that his natural human mind had revolted from the idea of the impending destruction of the countryside. It may well be, he thought with fear and awe, that this is God's signal judgment on the people for their sins. Mairi-daughter-of-Eoghann-Gasda he might have chosen out of the whole parish for the type and ensample of female virtue. Reared in the strictest forms of true religion, she had to all seeming lived a worthy child of her father, chaste, modest, keeping herself at home. On her father's death she had cheerfully and without complaint assumed the burden of supporting the cailleach his mother, and had in all things faithfully performed her duty until now. Maighstir Sachairi thought he could see how the hand and purpose of God might have led him that day to the shocking discovery that *even such a one as she* was the bondslave of concupiscence and carnal lust and secretly in flagrant sin. Nothing less than such a thing as outraged him in his very being could have wakened him out of his blindness. Now at least he could not be ignorant that sin in its ugliest shapes was about and prowling; and maybe the timely discovery had saved him on the brink of opposing himself to the will of God.

For he was unable any longer to be reassured by the seeming uprightness of his people. If such sin as that of Mairi-of-Eoghann-Gasda was scarcely heard of among them, yet sin had many forms; had he not but now seen into his own heart? He had been a blind guide, and now for what he could tell the whole parish might be full of such sin as his— of all sin the most offensive to God, veritably Sin itself, for it consisted in a heart and mind turned away towards creatures. Truly, Maighstir Sachairi thought, it may well be God's will to punish this people, for while they honoured Him with their lips their hearts may have been far from Him.

This disposed him to reflect with shame on his conduct towards the other ministers. It may be I have greatly wronged my brethren, he thought. I have held them guilty in my mind of conspiring with cruel men and wicked tyrants to oppress and rob their people, in my heart I have called them hirelings, false shepherds, betrayers and forsakers of their flocks; and thus I have hastily and arrogantly presumed to judge them. But my brethren, it may be, are not as I am, a judger of matters according to the fleshly counsels of my own heart. They may not have gone astray after the desires of their natural minds and therefore God may have opened up His purposes to them when He has most justly hidden them from me. Maighstir Sachairi was overtaken by remorse and he thought: I have wronged my brethren, I must humble myself before them.

3

Thinking so, he happened for the first time to raise his eyes a little. Not far away a man's head and shoulders were to be seen above the top of a dyke. The man was standing very still, and his eyes were looking straight at Maighstir Sachairi.

It was a moment before their glance brought Maighstir Sachairi to himself, but gradually it came to him where he was and what he had been doing. He was to draw himself together and continue on his way, for he realised how conspicuous and question-inspiring a figure he must have made. But even in the retreating edges of his preoccupation he had

sensed something unusual in the air of the figure behind the
dyke. He looked at him under his brows with attention. The
eyes were looking straight at Maighstir Sachairi. Even from
the head and shoulders it could be told the whole body stood
in a tense or strained attitude. Maighstir Sachairi felt he knew
the emotion of which the man exhibited the signs, and looked
more closely, searching in his mind for the name of it. Then
—it was manifest! The man was in a state of *fear!*

Maighstir Sachairi was somewhat surprised when he saw
this, and was to turn his head to look for the cause. But at
once another strange sight met his eye. A few yards farther
away there was a gap in the dyke, and in the gap was a gate.
Behind the gate three men were standing in a row, side by
side. They too stood in attitudes of tension. The two nearer
were looking straight at Maighstir Sachairi. In the eyes of
one of them he observed the same strained look of apprehension. But the other was frowning and seemed to be angry.
The third man stood sideways to him and with his chin
raised was looking fixedly at something in the distance at the
other side of the glen.

Maighstir Sachairi raised his head.

It was a day in March, hard but not chilly. There were
clear patches of blue in the sky overhead. Even the most
distant objects looked sharp and distinct. Gleann Luachrach
spread away eastwards—a flat-bottomed glen at this part, with
a considerable stream winding through it. Trees isolated or in
groups stood here and there along its banks, their still leafless
branches looking dark and brittle. Brown-dark fields occupied
the whole of the glen bottom and extended far up the hillsides
wherever their slope was not too acute. In all directions were
dotted farms and habitations, houses, outbuildings and
bothans among clumps of trees.

What was very strange in the familiar scene was to perceive
that all the people were out of doors. Beside their houses, in
the fields, men and women and children, alone or in groups,
they were standing as if rooted to the ground, every head
turned and every eye fixed in the same direction. Some had
even climbed on the roofs to get a better view and were

perched there, looking under their hands. Maighstir Sachairi
turned again to the men near him who had been regarding
him so keenly, but they also had now turned their heads
away and were looking away at the hillside across the glen.
Maighstir Sachairi recovered from his surprise at suddenly
seeing every door-mouth, every knoll and point of vantage,
occupied by motionless figures, and looked where they were
looking.

High up on the opposite slope of the glen, above the line
where cultivation ended, a heavy belt of smoke was extending
itself before the wind. At one end it was thickened to a point;
there it surged about in dense grey masses mingled and shot
with the glow of flame. When it lifted a little now and then a
fiery patch gleamed out brightly. Suddenly a red point leaped
up in another part of the brown moor. There had been no
rain, the heather was dry and brittle, before the brisk wind
the fire ran forward at great speed, leaping in bright tongues
from tuft to tuft. Almost at once smoke obscured and dulled
it and another dense grey column extended itself along the
hillside. Maighstir Sachairi now perceived a number of figures
moving on the slope. They stopped. Another flame leaped
up. He could not believe his eyes; they were firing the heather.

" What in the world are they doing yonder?" he called out.

The man turned and looked at Maighstir Sachairi.

" It is the Black Foreigner," he said.

It has begun! thought Maighstir Sachairi, and put his horse
in motion towards the burning party.

CHAPTER THREE

THE Factor had said: " I will never be satisfeed till the Gaelic language and the Gaelic people will be extirpated root and branch out o' this estate; aye, out o' the Highlands of Scotland."

He was arrogant with wine when he said that, swaggering among his lawyerish acquaintance in the town. But he was not a man to make an empty boast, being in his cups. He hated the Gaelic people, the more because he hated them without cause. He could not hear their language without rage. It affected him like an insult; as if by speaking a language he did not understand they dared to remind him there was yet a part of their minds and lives he could not enter and dominate and at his pleasure take away. He would have them entirely at his mercy; not their possessions only, but their very being must be his to dispose of, to grant or withdraw at will. With less than such god-like power, his thirst was still unslaked. It was not so much that he loved as that he *needed* to bully them, to browbeat and threaten them. He needed to see their tears and fearful looks, to hear their supplications. To know he held their livelihoods and their possessions in the hollow of his hand, to know they knew it, to have the power to alarm them with a look; that was an intoxication. But he had only to hear them talking together in their own language —less, he had only to think of it—to feel baffled and furious. Perhaps he hated them for their very defencelessness, for being at his mercy. But he was not a person to know this, though he was subtle. He only knew he hated them and that the mere existence of the Gaelic language inflamed him to fury, as if it cast in his face the limits of his power, as if it defied his authority, which must be paramount, and allowed

them to escape him after all. Therefore he had set his mind
on their destruction, and the more he knew they escaped him
in their being, and could not even understand the words in
which he expressed his hatred and contempt, the more his
fury against them knew no bounds.

One thing only threatened to baulk him of his perfect
vengeance. Unlike his fellow-ministers, Maighstir Sachairi
had refused to be his tool. Maighstir Sachairi had refused
to urge his people to submission and threaten all who
made resistance with the damnation of their souls. He
had taken the people's part and publicly defied him. There
was something here that puzzled the Factor even while it
angered him. He was not used to ministers who, having
received a living by the bounty of his master and theirs, would
not accept more from the same quarter to take their orders.
He could not see how Maighstir Sachairi thought to advantage
himself by acting as he did—and it was characteristic of him
that he never for a moment supposed Maighstir Sachairi
might not be acting for his own advantage. (For not only was
he in the habit of attributing self-interest to all men as their
sole motive, as it was the only one he admitted to himself,
but he had never hitherto encountered any exception to minis-
terial venality.) However, the Factor was not a man to ignore
a challenge to his power, and he had not halted in the execu-
tion of his plans. It was for Maighstir Sachairi now to show
what he would do.

Maighstir Sachairi sat on his horse looking up at the fires
on the slope above him. In the softening of the wind their
crackling could be distinctly heard. So too could the voices
of the figures moving purposefully on the hillside. His eyes
looked thoughtful, abstracted. But his restless hand expressed
perplexity or indecision, fingering on the reins.

" This is a terrible thing, Factor," he said. " It will be fair
ruination." His tone too was hesitant.

The Factor curved the lips in his black beard and showed
the edges of his teeth in a haughty smile. " Yea?" he said in
a bantering, provocative tone.

Maighstir Sachairi did not appear to have heard. " A fell

ruination," he repeated as if to himself. Without taking his eyes from the blazing hillside he went on, " Ye ken how to be cruel, Factor. Ye couldna have chosen a worser time. This spring of all springs! There's hardly a blade o' feeding, and the poor beasts have naething but the grass that will be sprouting out among the heather yonder. After sic a falloisg as ye are giving us there's just the two things that can happen, Factor: either the beasts maun starve to daith, or else the folk maun roup them—and ye canna help kennin' there's no price at all to be gotten for beasts this season. It's a most serious business, this; and the end o' it will be ruination whatever."

The Factor drew his brows together into a frown. " Ye're forgettin'," he said grimly, " the girse will be a' the better o' this. Wait ye a whilie an' ye'll see what grand girse it'll be yet."

Maighstir Sachairi looked at him. He knew what the Factor meant. He meant that after the heather had been burnt away the grass would grow more freely, and at a later season would make an excellent pasture—*for sheep*. It was a reference to the Factor's intention to clear the people from the glen. Maighstir Sachairi knew he was being dared to his face.

He looked at the man, the familiar strong figure sitting straight-backed on his horse. As always, he was struck by his appearance of health—the look of robust wholesomeness that in such a man as the Factor was accustomed to make a faintly unpleasant impression on him. The skin was white on his broad brow and ruddy over his cheekbones. The jet black hair of his head and his full beard was glossy with health. His rather thick lips were deep red. His teeth when he smiled were strong and regular and white. Just now his black eyes turned on Maighstir Sachairi with a bold question.

Maighstir Sachairi turned away. He let his eyes travel over the fields and houses, the familiar scene, and one who knew him might have detected in his air an unwonted dejection.

" It maun be a long while since the glen was a desert without people," he said after a little, as if reflecting aloud. " Did it ever come across your mind, Factor, that since ever there was people in this glen at all, they have been the same people as is here the-day? It's a thing I whiles think upon; and it's a remarkable thing that as far as we ken there was never any hereabouts forbye just the forebears o' them that ye see there now. At the time the first o' them came, all this country would be nothing but a desert, there would be neither house nor bigging, just the desert and the beasts o' the desert. And if it's now as bonny a spot as ye will see in Scotland it's just that they have warstled and contended wi' the desert, every generation o' them, till at last they brought it under the spade and the plough. There's no' a field o' it they havena conquered from the bog and the heather; there's no' a tree they havena planted. And for houses, it's themselves that bigged every four walls. Forbye that, they were aye ready and able to stand up for what was their own against enemies, and them that were over them they aye defended with their lives and keepit them in their possessions. Mind ye it's a remarkable thing, but I doubt if there's a folk in Scotland that has a more ancient or a better-earned right to the place they bide in."

Maighstir Sachairi stopped speaking. The Factor had been regarding him quizzically, with his black eyes. He was thinking, The minister is changing his tune! The idea came into his mind that maybe Maighstir Sachairi's object had been to hold off for a higher price.

He gave a laugh. "That's a' bye wi', Maister Zachary. What need they care that has the Parliament o' London at their backs! Man dae ye ken they dinna gie a bodle doon yonder for your swoords and your daiggers and your speaks aboot richts. They juist sit doon and pass an Act—and there's an end o' your richts to this and richts to that."

He heaved a sigh loud with simulated regret. "Ah weel," said he in mock sentimentality, "Auld times, Maister Sachairi! Auld times! Weel, we've haen a fine crack."

As if recollecting himself, he became serious and looked about him, alert. He frowned. "I'll bid ye a guid day," he said curtly, and pulling his rein, wheeled and put his horse to a trot.

After a time Maighstir Sachairi withdrew his eyes from following the Factor. He cleared his throat and, touching his horse into motion, rode away. Riding slowly, his head began to droop forward till his chin rested on his breast. The horse turned aside up the short track to his house; Maister Sachairi came to himself finding a lank, black-haired man holding his bridle and looking inquisitively into his face, with the strange " mixed " look of the dead-eyed. He at once swung down and stepped to the ground. " Take the saddle off her, Lachlan," he said with assumed casualness, walking away to the house, while the man stared after him.

He closed the door of the room behind him, threw off his plaid and went and sat down in his chair. Then stooping forward, he lifted two or three turfs of peat and dropped them on the fire. He rose with a gesture and went and stood at the window. Taking out his snuffbox, he applied the snuff to his nose, pursing up his lips. Then clasping his hands behind his back he looked out of the window, and began to look anxious and preoccupied and to frown into the distance.

Following the shattering discovery of Mairi-of-Eoghann-Gasda's sin, coming so close on the heels of reflections so devastating to his mental peace, the meeting with the Factor had completed his discomposure and made him comprehend how utterly those events had altered the relation in which he stood to that man and his works. So long as he saw this calamity which threatened his people as no more than a wrong conceived in the proud hearts of wicked men, so long he had been able to act with vigour and decision, for he saw his duty clearly. If his people required to be defended from cruel men and oppressors, that was a duty he could accept with readiness, for he did not fear a tyrant. But meeting the Factor at the very moment when he did not know whether he ought to regard him as the instrument of Divine vengeance, he had found himself deprived of all decision; he had sat before him helpless and confused. For he no longer knew in which direction his duty lay, or whether the man ought to be opposed or submitted to. Maighstir Sachairi recalled to mind his halting and equivocal tone, and was ashamed. He began to wonder what the Factor had thought, whether he had observed that a change had taken place in him. The Factor had expected to be taken up where the matter had rested at Dùn Eachainn; and he found instead one who had nothing to say to him but to address him with large phrases. He *must* have noticed. Maighstir Sachairi blushed, thinking of the miserable part he had played. Is it possible, he thought, that I seemed to *plead—I,* with such a man as the Factor! He remembered the Factor's eyes, fixed on his face with a bold, mocking expression. And he thought in a sudden start of anger: If only I had my strength on me! would I not outface him! I am Sachairi Wiseman, I am stronger than he!

At this point Maighstir Sachairi drew himself up with a sudden quick movement and cast a startled glance aside. He had all at once realised where his thoughts had carried him. Only that day, having mercy on his blindness and stiffness of neck, God had vouchsafed in a singular and startling manner to open his eyes and save him on the very brink of opposing His will. And he—still unrecovered from his alarm and dismay—had already relapsed in his heart into sinful opposition to His purpose and condemned, despised and arrogantly put down in his proud mind the instrument of His correction. Maighstir Sachairi was aghast. He thought: If this terrible thing is from God I ought rather to have been exercising myself to submission. If He will utterly destroy my people in just recompense for their sins and my own, and because our secret hearts have been far from Him, it is for me to quell the resistance of my rebellious human mind and make humble my heart before His chastisement.

He began to recall a day in which he had had no need to be reminded of his duty, nor spared himself in its performance. Twenty years before, Maighstir Sachairi came to Gleann Luachrach a young man of twenty-seven, full of zeal for the service of God. He found it given over to vanity; singing and dancing, contests of wit or manly prowess, were the principal enjoyment of the people. But his zeal was not little. Any man that was for the Devil's amusements found his flinty face never relaxed against him. He did not spare his flesh. He was so active on the foot of duty that he seemed to be everywhere at once; breathing out anathemas, exhorting, pleading, thundering. In the end he had them on their knees weeping and crying to God to avert the visitation of His wrath. The Holy Ghost swept through Gleann Luachrach with the sough of the whirlwind, so that any that were without the changed heart hid their faces and kept peace. Even Fearchar the Poet had been confounded and silenced.

But another day had come for Maighstir Sachairi. By degrees and insensibly that pristine zeal had left him, for the tool rusts and grows blunt lacking its proper use. He had grown unwatchful. He smiled and nodded. He waved his hand in a genial curve. He pushed out his lips and made kissing noises bending over gurling infants . . . Maighstir Sachairi brushed off some snuff that had tumbled on his waistcoat, and as he did so felt its comfortable curves reproach him. He saw himself at that moment like the ruins of an apostle, and he thought, How are the mighty fallen! He clasped his hands behind him and sighed profoundly, for the zealous fires of youth.

Maighstir Sachairi fell now to pondering that youth, and calling back to his recollection one by one the acts of his zeal and service, began to be filled again with the pride of its triumphs. He breathed deeply, and the heart throbbed in his breast. He felt himself as a young man again, scoured and purged to be the vessel of the Lord. He remembered how he had been a warrior for God in those days, how he had warstled with the Devil, how with parched mouth had groaned and sweated in grips with the flesh—*Down dog!*—and trampled it underfoot.

And now at last thinking he saw clearly that God had reserved him for yet another service he began to be eager for the conflict, he began to long to suffer again at His hands, to be tried to the uttermost and buffeted and torn asunder. He cried out in his soul, God, let me bear it. Try me in the fire. Scourge me; let me be racked and broken, utterly broken down and emptied altogether. Lord, I accept it, I offer myself . . . But suddenly with an awful, more-than-daylight clearness there appeared before his mind what it was that he must suffer; the desolation of his familiar, pleasant home, fire, ruin, the faces of his people transfixed with dread and horror, their doom and endless banishment . . . The eyes in his blenched face stared into the distance. He shuddered. Suddenly he put up both his hands and bowed his face into their palms.

CHAPTER FOUR

THE sun of spring rested brightly along a hill ridge on which the green points of grass were again pushing out among charred heather roots and boulders blackened by a recent passage of fire. A stony track ran over the round top of the ridge and dipped sharply into the glen beyond. The Factor, approaching from the south, drew up his horse on the summit and looked about him. First his eye looked carefully over the ground at the fresh springing grass, and he must have been pleased at what he saw for he gave a grunt of satisfaction. Then he raised his head. Before him and on either side the ridges and hill shoulders passed behind each other into haze and distance. Here and there were hills; some pointed, standing alone, others of a rounded irregular bulk. To the west the land began to rise into a range, high and massive. The sky was light blue and almost cloudless. Sitting his horse on the summit, their shadow lying on the track before him, the Factor was conscious of the spring sun's kindly heat warming his back, while his face and hands were touched by the small wind breathing faintly chill from the north.

He gave a slight, involuntary cough, as if something had irritated his throat. Wrinkling up his nose, he began turning his head this way and that, sniffing the air. There was borne to him unmistakably the acrid smell of smoke; and immediately he coughed again. Touching his horse, he rode forward a little and looked down into the glen.

Because of the faintness of the wind it lay there undisturbed. Down there everything was obscured and hidden by the smoke. The whole glen was filled with it, and neither fields nor houses nor even the flames could be seen under its dense blanket. The Factor looked a while at the grey pall moving slightly with an undulating motion like the sea, and a smile played about his mouth. He became alert, and turning his head a little, inclined his ear and listened intently. Away down in the glen bottom he thought he heard the noise of some commotion, a confused noise in which could be detected faint sounds like distant shouting or shrieking. The Factor's smile broadened. He lifted his head and with his eyes half closed listened as if to something more than agreeable: on his face an expression of triumph and satisfaction.

He was interrupted by a sound near him. Some man was climbing up the track from the glen and as he approached he was taken every now and then by a fit of coughing. The Factor turned his horse and riding back a short distance took up his position in the shadow cast by a rocky protuberance which made a landmark at the summit of the track. The coughing came nearer. A head and shoulders appeared. When he reached the summit he was a tallish, thin man wrapped in a plaid, the edge of which he was holding over his mouth. Not noticing the Factor in the shadow he halted and turned round to take his breath and look behind.

When he was to continue on his way the Factor rode out and planted himself in his path. The man started back, finding a horse almost above him, and the plaid-edge fell from his opened mouth. He looked up, blinking, and one of his eyes was white and dead. He was Maighstir Sachairi's "man."

The Factor laughed, recognising him.

"Ye're far traivelled the-day, Lachlan."

A confused and guilty look came into the man's face. He looked aside. "My sister she wass live in Gleann Mór," he said apologetically, as if he had been caught in a fault.

"Weel that's a' richt, Lachlan. I hae nae objection I assure ye."

The man did not appear to be reassured by the Factor's hearty voice. He kept his eyes lowered and seemed ill at ease. The Factor looked him over. By and by an amused twinkle came into his eye.

"An' hoo *is* your sister, Lachlan?"

The man coloured and became even more confused. He looked at his feet and shuffled, not knowing what to say. At last, " She wass not be so weel the-day," he mumbled.

The Factor took him up. " Nae weel?" he said with pretended concern, while his eye twinkled. " Man, that's awfu'. I'm maist sorry to hear that." He looked at the man, enjoying the discomfort his banter was causing him.

Then his tone changed. He became serious. " Lachlan!" he said in a low voice, in an urgent, confidential tone, " Yon thing we were speakin' aboot—are ye mindin'?"

The man looked up. His confusion had vanished. He surveyed the Factor with a mixture of shrewdness and servility, his good eye half closed. Then, " I wass be minding fine," he said.

The Factor surveyed him in return. " I wonder."

" I'll juist try ye—," he went on. " Ye hae been doon yonder " (indicating with a movement of his head the smoke-filled Gleann Mór). " Ye wad see something. Noo than, Lachlan, juist ye tell me, what was it that ye saw?"

The man continued to regard the Factor with a now almost impudent, calculating look. He took his time to reply.

" I wass see the Shudgment of God," he said.

" Fine! " cried the Factor, delighted. " ' The Shudgment o' Gode! ' I see ye mind it! And, ' It's an ill thing to counter the will o' Gode; them that gangs agin Him is aye punished ' —mind ye dinna forget that! "

The man's eye was now so screwed up as to be almost closed; he was regarding the Factor with barely-disguised insolence.

" ' And them that wass do His will iss be rewarded,' " he said as if meaningly. " You wassna forgot that, Maighstir Byars?"

For a single instant the Factor seemed to try to recall something. " Oh aye, aye! " he burst out with sudden alacrity in a hearty voice. " Na, na! I didna forget. ' Them that does His will aye gets their reward '—that's richt, Lachlan! Man, but ye're guid at mindin'! "

" Ah weel, guid day tae ye, Lachlan! " he said, bringing

the conversation to an end by putting his horse in motion and forcing the man to step hastily aside off the track. " Mind noo an' no forget your wordies! " he called over his shoulder.

He rode forward and began the descent. Before long the smoke was getting into his throat and he covered his nose and mouth. Behind the plaid-edge a small, sardonic smile began to play about his lips. He had remembered the man's expression. He thought, So his sister was " no sae weel the-day "! Gode! That's a way to put it!

He looked down into the grey, uneasy blanket made by the smoke of blazing houses in Gleann Mór. And his eyes looking over the plaid-edge hardened.

The man called Lachlan remained looking after the Factor when he had gone. His look was sly and calculating. He went forward and stood a while looking down the road he had taken into the glen. Then he turned and cast his eye up to the heavens. The sun had begun to decline towards the west. Adjusting his plaid about his shoulders because the cold wind was freshening out of the north he set off with his rapid, awkward gait towards the south.

Several hours later he was not more than ten miles away. He was leaning against a rock in a deep barren cleft among high hills. All the time the weather had been worsening rapidly. The north wind had freshened to a half gale. Blown before it the cold rain-clouds had spread southwards over the whole sky. An hour before while descending a rocky path in the gathering dusk he had stepped on a loose stone and fallen steeply. When he rose a sharp pain shot up from his ankle and he gave a yelping cry with the pain. Now he leant against the rock and it was already so dark that by the pale streaks where the clouds thinned it was barely possible to discern the shapes of the hills. The wind made a shrilling noise along the hillsides. Now and then the rain descended in sharp, drenching showers driven by the wind. He was chilled and his clothes were sodden. Brushing out of his eyes the water trickling from the dank hair plastered on his forehead he looked about despondently into the gloom.

After a while he attempted to proceed, groaning and hirpling. There was there a place where two tracks diverged: one that ran straight ahead led to Gleann Luachrach, and that was his road; the other turned off to the left and climbed up the hillside eastwards. He stopped there and considered the ten miles between him and the end of his journey. Then he considered the four miles to the head of the other glen. The thought of the snug houses there and how he would be able to warm and rest himself and pass the night decided him. He turned to the left and began the ascent. Darkness had almost completely descended. Behind and above him the wind rushed southward, shrieking. He made his slow way bent almost double, groping with his hands and helping himself on by the rocks and boulders that lay above the track.

Before he reached the summit the moon had risen behind the clouds and its rays coming down through the lighter spaces made pale, irregular patches that moved among the hills. The wind was lifting. As he made the descent he was stifling little cries of pain. But above the pain of his ankle he was conscious now of another. Since the night before he had not eaten, and his hunger began to gnaw him. There was a house yonder, the nearest to the head of the glen, and in it at one time or another he had often eaten and passed the night. That was his objective; as he made his painful way there began to float before his mind with a strange warm clearness visions of the meals he had taken there. The host, tenant of a small farm, was a solid, comfortable man. He saw him rising rosy-faced from the fire to greet him, bid him welcome. " A Lachlan! May it be a happy journey that brought you, worthy man! " And then immediately the customary, " Wife! here is Lachlan of Maighstir Sachairi come to put past the night with us! Put before him what you have in the house and let us see how they can eat in Gleann Luachrach! " He saw the children's rosy faces, the hospitable firelight on the cheery faces of the guests gathered round, the shy daughters putting the food on the table for him. Most of all and above all, with a strange clearness of corporeal reality, he saw the food. He saw porridge steaming in the wooden bowl. On his plate he saw the small and tasty trout of Loch an Laoigh Bhallaich. He saw butter, a tottering pile of oaten cakes and bannocks, the home-made cheese. Little wisps of steam were rising from a heap of eggs beside him. He saw all faintly through frothy cream cascading from a wide jug-mouth. And a voice saying, " Stretch your hand, Lachlan! "

He raised his eyes and in the pale, diffused moonlight he saw the place before him—and was it a window glimmering hospitably through the clump of trees! At last! He slid forward down the little slope, dislodging stones, and somehow splashed through the burn, catching his breath as the icy water swirled round his calves. Helping himself by the low branches he hopped and struggled through the densely growing trees and burst out at the other side with his mouth already open for a hail . . .

His mouth stayed open. His eye goggled. He closed his mouth slowly. Then he gave his head a sudden shake, and drawing his breath opened his mouth again to hail. But the sound was arrested in his throat. He stared again.

Gradually he knew that he saw what he saw. The house was a smoking shell. The pale moonlight went through the gaping window-holes and lay across the smoking heaps that had been the roof and the interior. The gable had fallen out. The air was filled with a sickening stench of burning. He now noticed that even the branch he was still holding on to to support himself was charred.

With the realisation, the man Lachlan swayed and clutched the branch more strongly. Suddenly deprived of the immediacy of anticipation which had supported him, he sagged and a sound like a sob came from his throat. He continued to stare in a kind of helplessness at the scene of desolation the emerging moon displayed more solidly every moment. In the stress of his sensations of pain and hunger he had forgotten the things he had seen that day. They crowded back into his mind. Now he knew why the Factor's face was towards the north when he met him!

After a time he began to make an attempt to move away. But now he was past walking. He seemed to be in a sort of stupor, and whether from the cold and his sodden clothes, or because of the shock he had received, he was attacked by violent fits of shivering and trembling. By the help of the low branches he was able to reach the end of the line of trees. Then gathering his strength, he made a hop and reached the low dyke, over which he leaned and rested himself. There were the burnt-out ruins of byre and stable and out-houses. He could almost see the bare-legged children driving in the cows with their calves. He heard their cries . . .

Several hours later he had covered two miles. The rain had long ceased and the clouds dispersed. The moon shone brightly. On all sides, on the receding slopes and in the broad strath-floor, it shone on the smoking ruins of habitations, crofts and farms and bothans. The perpetual sickening smell of burning lay on his stomach and affected him with a mounting nausea.

He saw that he was close to the churchyard. The church was the only building in the glen with a roof remaining. The gravestones stood looking white and unreal at the ends of their black shadows. He was looking dully at the white gravestones and the bulk of the church when it began to penetrate to his numbed consciousness that he was hearing a sound. Above the continuous noise of the burn water he was hearing a faint undulating sound like a bairn wailing. Then he heard as it were low voices. He began to feel fear: the sounds were coming from the graves. He looked about among them with an uneasy, apprehensive shiver. Suddenly, terror struck through him and rooted him to the spot. His eyes goggled and bulged forward in his head. He shook in every limb.

A figure had risen from one of the graves and was standing beside the gravestone. A woman. The moon shone white on the deathly face, the long hair hung in disorder, through the hair the eyes looked with a wild, unearthly gleam. It raised its arm and began to extend it, slowly, in his direction, the finger pointing. His knees smote against each other. A shaking sound trembled from his lips. Suddenly the thing moved— shrieked—. He saw no more. Leaping backwards, he came

down on his damaged ankle and with a loud cry of pain and
terror tumbled in a heap.

" Who is there?"

Hearing the human voice, he raised his head. A man was
standing inside the churchyard wall looking from side to side.
Almost at the same moment the man caught sight of him
lying on the ground and stepped across the wall.

" Who is it?" he said, approaching.

" I am Lachlan MacMhuirich from Gleann Luachrach,"
said Maighstir Sachairi's man in a faint voice, not yet recovered from his fright.

The man came and stood beside him.

" You cried out. Are you hurt?"

Lachlan MacMhuirich pointed. " I have broken my foot."

" My grief! I am sorry for that," said the man. He was
silent a moment, considering. " I will carry you then; it is no
worse in there than it is here. Are you able to stand on your
one foot?"

Helping Lachlan MacMhuirich to an upright position, he
lifted him on his back and walked stooping towards the
churchyard. When they got over the wall there was a little
shelter made of pieces of wood resting one end on the wall
and the other on a gravestone, and blankets laid over the
wood. The woman caught up the child and stood some paces
away, looking and peering at Lachlan MacMhuirich a little
wildly.

" Herself was thinking you were the Black Foreigner," the
man said, rather breathless, lowering the other off his back.
" I'm afraid she will not be the same in her mind, poor
creature—"

Letting Lachlan MacMhuirich to the ground, he helped
him to crawl inside the shelter where there was some sodden
straw. Then he went on his knees at the mouth of the shelter
and prepared to render what aid he could.

" My sorrow!" he said in a pitiful tone. " That's a bad
foot you have there, poor man."

But for the other man one need was still uppermost. His
voice came from the shadow faintly.

"For Christ's sake—if you have food—"

The man sat back, and he no longer made an effort not to look dejected. "Ourselves have had nothing all the day," he said in a hollow, despondent voice. He bowed his head. "Never has any man gone hungry from Donnchadh Mac-na-Ceardadh's door. Never—"

A little later without raising his head he said in his hollow tone, "You are from Gleann Luachrach. How is it with them there?"

But Lachlan MacMhuirich had passed the edge of his endurance. From pain, hunger, and exhaustion, he was falling into a swoon.

"It is—well—" he managed to say, slipping.

"God be praised!" he heard Donnchadh Mac-na-Ceardadh's voice say. And then—receding—"All here are wiped out."

CHAPTER FIVE

"A LL wiped out? Did Lachlan Cearbach say wiped out?"
The miller shouted through the din and clatter, looking
incredulously at the figure standing in the doorway.

The man nodded his head.

"His very words," he shouted back. "He was there and
he saw it."

They stared at each other. The miller went and turned a
lever and the clatter subsided. Coming out into the light, he
was a middle-aged man of a portly bulk of body, white from
his trade. An apron of sacking, whitened in use, extended
downwards from the folds of his chin over his belly and hung
out in front of his knees, and the white dust of the meal was
sprinkled over his blue bonnet, his fair hair, and among the
stubble on his plump cheeks. He bore himself like a man of
character and substance, a serious man, deliberate in thought
and action. Standing in the doorway, he looked very gravely
at the other, frowning in thought, but giving no sign that he
had just received the most alarming news except that several
times a scant eyebrow and the corner of his mouth twitched,
as though a slight involuntary spasm passed over his features.
Looking steadily, he rubbed one palm slowly up and down a
massive, dusty forearm.

He said shortly, "We must see Iain."

At no great distance a little house sat on the pleasant
southward slope, a neat little dwelling, snugly thatched, seeming to display its newness in the sun. It was to just such a
house that a young man would bring his bride.

It did in fact contain a young wife, and, happier still, a new
mother. She was then dividing her time between the cradle
and a pot that swung above the fire, and now and again

[57]

standing still in the room for pride of the house that in those parts was the gift of friends to a young pair that married, or touching with self-conscious fingers the white currachd on her head out of happiness that she was a wife. The sun came through the low window and fell across the cradle. She went there and lifted up the tiny creature so that he lay across her arms, and stooping, began to shower on him kisses and endearments.

But she happened to raise her head and to glance through the window, and her face changed. Her eyes watched the two figures hurrying past below the house; with an instinctive movement she caught up the bundle to her breast. She had gone white to the lips. When they had passed from sight she gave one startled look about her, put down the infant in the cradle, and without waiting to straighten herself caught her skirts and ran straight out of the house. At the door she put her hand above her eyes and gave one look after them, then catching up her skirts ran like the wind in the opposite direction.

There was a large field on the slope nearby, and the corn just showing green above the ground. There were two men at the farther side. They had their backs to her and they were shouting and brandishing sticks to drive out some reluctant cattle that had invaded the corn. There were some young lads and boys with them helping them.

"Fionnlagh! Fionnlagh!" she cried, coming up to the low wall.

One of the cattle broke back into the field and they redoubled their activity, running with sticks in the air, shouting.

She put her two hands up to her mouth and high-pitching her voice made the call travel across the field. "A Fionnlagh!"

A young man turned round and smiled in her direction, almost closing his eyes as he turned into the sun. He saw her and began to walk towards her across the field. She raised her arm and waved him on, her hand describing urgent circles, and always she cast an agitated glance over her shoulder and back again at him approaching. He came on at

his leisure, smiling at her, with what seems the obstinate dull-
ness of people at a distance, unable to sense her mood.

He came to the other side of the dyke. " Anna, love," he
said, hardly at all in question and wholly in endearment,
smiling down on her. Then he noticed her white looks.
" Anna, love! " he repeated, now with sudden urgency in his
tone. " What——?"

But her agitation kept her speechless, she could only point,
then look at him. He raised his head, his keen eyes of the
mountain man narrowed, searching the glen in the direction
her hand had pointed.

" I see nothing. Anna, what is it for God's sake?"

" Fionnlagh—" She found her voice; her hand pointed.
" Do you not see him? The miller—look! "

He looked again.

" I see the miller certainly. But Annag, what is frightening
about Tormod Bàn?"

" But, Fionnlagh—" She was distressed by his inability to
understand at once, without words. " He had—— there was
—there was *calamity* in his face."

" Calamity in his face? Annag—you——" He seemed inclined to be amused. He turned to the other man who had
been with him, who had crossed the field and at that moment
came up behind, a tall young man, and by the great resem-
blance between them a brother. " Cailean, here is a silly lass
that has been frightened by the miller. She says the worthy
man's face frightened her."

The other gave a slow, half-indulgent smile as if he supposed he had come up when there was some jest between the
pair. But he no sooner glanced at the young woman than he
seemed struck by something. "The miller—" he said. "Where
is the miller?"

The two figures were still at no great distance; in the bottom
of Gleann Luachrach filled with spring sunshine they were
conspicuous enough. The miller with his heavy belly rolled
a little in his gait. With his fists clenched and working his
bare arms he laboured forward resolutely. The much slighter
man at his side hurried to keep up the pace.

The young men on the slope watched them, eyes narrowed in the sun.

The one that was called Cailean spoke, reflectively. " In his great haste," he said. Then, " Maybe the lass was right, Fionnlagh! " He watched. The other with him should be a Sisealach, by the jumping gait of him."

After a little—" If they turn up to Iain's now, this means news. Bad news, I would say."

They were watching the hurrying figures intently now, with a kind of suppressed eagerness. The young man Fionnlagh was watching their every movement with such grim intentness as if they had been enemies, his head thrust forward, his mouth set. He had gone slightly pale.

" They are to turn! " Cailean cried in a high, strained voice. " Yes! they are turning! God help us, I wonder what this is! " Without looking at the other two he vaulted over the low wall and set off at full speed. They saw him pause, shout something to a man that emerged from a doorway, wave his hand, and run on; and the other having turned and called something into the house, ran too. Two women were all at once outside the door, looking under their hands. In a moment a third man emerged between them and set off running.

The young man Fionnlagh had climbed over the wall. He looked down at Anna. " You know Cailean," he said, affecting a light tone, and with a gesture of the hand after the running figures. But when she turned, the numb and wordless terror in her eyes disconcerted him. He faltered and went no farther. " But I will go myself and hear if there is anything—" he said, now attempting no more than the matter-of-fact, and his own face rather pale. He looked at her again, seemed to hesitate, then without a word scrugged his bonnet and setting his face forward, walked away. For a short distance he tried to maintain a casual bearing, but by degrees his pace became more rapid. Several times he glanced back at her over his shoulder, and always he was walking more quickly. At last with a final glance behind he threw away all pretence and broke into a run. She remained rooted to the spot, staring after him, but as if she saw nothing. But when he began to run, she clasped her hands together.

The miller and his companion had turned aside where there was a short slope leading up to a squat, hut-like building. Near one gable, wisps of smoke were rising through the thatch, and smoke was trickling out also under the broad, low doorway. From inside came the clear ringing sounds, the blunted bell-notes of hammer ringing upon anvil. The two came up the slope breathless. Near the smithy door a rather surly-looking swarthy man was leaning against the wall, smoking. He turned his head and at the first sight of their faces his eyebrows rose. He took a step away from the wall and caught a bare-legged boy that was playing there by the collar. " Be off, now," he said. " Your mother wants you." He turned the boy round so that he faced down the glen, brought his palm sharply against his buttocks, and the startled child shot away without a look behind at the topmost speed of his small legs. The man returned and leant his shoulder lazily against the wall. He folded his arms, crossed one foot over the other, and regarded the newcomers with an impassive stare.

The two came up to the smithy door, and their first word was drowned in a sudden furious sizzling. The smith was bending down holding something with long tongs into a pail of water, presenting the top of his bonnet. He noticed a darkness fall and looked up. Although their faces were in shadow he at once sensed something unusual in the two figures blocking the door. He took the iron out of the pail and threw it down. Coming to the door, he leant his hands on the ridge of the closed lower portion. The others stepped back a pace or two. He looked first into one face then into the other.

" What news?" he said, the look of concern on their faces beginning to be reflected in his own.

The smith was not a tall man, but his breadth filled the doorway. His neck and throat, and his arms, bare from below the shoulder, were nervous and muscular rather than thick or massive; where they were not smeared with soot and grime the skin was very white. His hair was black, but the square, hard beard was a little brown in front as if from frequent scorching. His eyes were dark blue, in expression frank and candid; just now surprisingly youthful and ingenuous, looking out of his grimy face with an expression of half-bewildered enquiry. The miller had said in a breathless voice, panting, " It has come at last! "

" What has come?" he asked.

The stout miller was labouring to recover his breath. He nodded across at the other man. " Ailean Sisealach can tell. it."

Just then the young man Cailean came running up, and close behind him the two men he had called out of their house as he passed. They came to a stand beside the miller and his companion, their breathing sounding loud. At first they glanced at each of the others in turn, with quick movements of their heads from side to side, but noticing that both the miller and the smith were looking at Ailean Sisealach, they also fixed their eyes on him. The young husband Fionnlagh, the brother of Cailean, came up running, his face white nonetheless.

Ailean Sisealach seemed reluctant to begin. As if the eyes fixed on him expectantly made him uncomfortable, he kept his own averted.

He said, " Three days ago Lachlan MacMhuirich went away to visit his sister in Gleann Mór. To-day he came into my brother's house at Bad-an-Losguinn, having come through Bealach-an-Fhithich." He seemed to become embarrassed. " He was crawling on his belly and he was saying, as if he was dying, ' Food! food! For Christ's sake give me something to eat!' "

The smith waited a little, expecting him to proceed. " What was wrong with Lachlan Cearbach? Had he gone out of his mind?"

Ailean Sisealach slowly raised his eyes. " No," he said with a significant look. " He was hungry."

The smith wrinkled his brow. " I don't understand you. If he came from Gleann Mór it is no more than twenty or thirty miles. And if he came through Bealach-an-Fhithich he had been in Srath Meadhonach, and that is but ten. How then could he be hungry? Do you mean to say that nobody would give him food?"

The other was still looking at him solemnly. In the same significant tone he said, "I don't mean that exactly, Iain."

"Well what are you meaning, Ailean? Was there no food in all the houses of Gleann Mór and Srath Meadhonach?" The smith sounded incredulous.

"There was no food; and there was nothing else either." The same hesitation overcame Ailean Sisealach. He turned his head away and fixed his eyes on the distance over the heads of the little group about him. When he spoke again it was in a voice become small.

"There are no *people* in Gleann Mór and Srath Meadhonach."

The smith stared at him. In his eyes a fearful comprehension dawned. He repeated in a kind of stupefaction, "It has come at last, I understand now!" He struck his palm against his brow.

There was a chill silence. Everyone staring upon Ailean Sisealach, their faces blenched and rigid. Fionnlagh with a quick and sudden movement turned about, and, his head thrust forward and nostrils and eyes dilated, fists clenched by his sides, scanned the distance to eastward.

"Tell us now," said the smith in a toneless voice.

Aileann Sisealach made a gesture. "It seems he twisted his foot in Coire Fhearchair and turned aside to pass the night in Srath Meadhonach. And when he got there—" (he lifted his hands and let them drop to his sides)—"nothing but smoke and ruins."

"Were there no people left at all?"

The man's head drooped forward; he spoke in a low voice, staring at the ground. "No people at all." After a little— "But there was a man there—Donnchadh Mac-na-Ceardadh —Donnchadh Fada—"

Another man who appeared at that moment from somewhere heard the name. "Donnchadh Fada Mac-na-Ceardadh? I know him. He is the farmer at Druim Beag in Srath Meadhonach. A godly man, and a wealthy one. He has twenty breeding cows, that man . . ."

He stopped, seeing Ailean Sisealach's face, turned towards him over his shoulder.

" He *was* the farmer at Druim Beag. When Lachlan Cearbach saw him he was taking shelter in the churchyard, and he had nothing in the world but his plaid and a bundle of wet straw. His wife was with him, and she was out of her mind. She was wandering about among the graves, and every shadow she saw she thought it was the Black Foreigner. She was pointing with her finger, like this, and crying out, ' Oh! there's Byars; there's Byars! ' "

" Out of her mind! God's pity on us! " cried the smith.

" In the morning it seems they had discovered that some of the people were not with the rest, and Damnable Donald with the other tools of the Black Foreigner came back to root them out. They had with them the minister—what is his name? the long thin one—Maighstir Tormod; they had Maighstir Tormod with them and it was he that found Donnchadh Fada and Lachlan Cearbach and Donnchadh Fada's wife in the churchyard. He started to shout, " Here they are! Here they are! " The officers came, and Damnable Donald took the sticks and blankets they had for a shelter and threw them over the churchyard wall, cursing and swearing in the presence of the minister and the minister taking no heed. It appears they were angry at having to come so far; only for trash, they said. Donnchadh Fada was begging to be left because his wife was out of her mind. But one of them said he would manage her and began chasing her among the graves, and then he caught her and began dragging her by the hair, she shrieking and throwing herself down and screaming at the pitch of her voice. Donnchadh Fada gave a shout and ran and knocked him down with a blow of his fist. So four or five of them jumped on Donnchadh Fada and began to tie his arms behind him with ropes, he standing and not resisting them and saying: ' God forgive me! God forgive me! ' They were to tie Lachlan Cearbach also but when they knew he was from Gleann Luachrach, they left him. But when they were moving away Damnable Donald came behind Donnchadh Fada on his horse and kicked him with his foot on his shoulder, calling him a son of Satan. And because his arms were tied with the ropes he could not rise and they had to get down and lift him up where he was lying on his face. Donnchadh Fada asked them in a quiet voice to wipe the blood out of his eyes and Damnable Donald did this with Donnchadh's own bonnet but saying it was more than he deserved. So they went, Donnchadh Mac-na-Ceardadh walking alone with his arms tied behind him and his face covered with blood, and one of them holding the woman in front of him on a horse, screaming, and Maighstir Tormod carrying the child."

The rumour of bad news had travelled quickly. Men in twos and threes had been coming up and silently joining the group. At this point an old grey-bearded man came up and pushed his way through the circle of men standing. He had not heard the story, but he had heard something, for he made straight for Ailean Sisealach in great agitation and caught him by the sleeve with a shaking hand.

" Caitriona," he said. He was breathless and could hardly speak. " How is she, my daughter Caitriona?"

Ailean Sisealach was overcome with confusion. He glanced about as if he would have fled, and made a movement of pulling his arm away. He could only stammer, " I . . . I don't know. If she was in Srath Meadhonach . . . I . . . I don't know. They are all gone now."

" Yes, yes! Srath Meadhonach! She is the wife of Eachann Donn of Baile Shimi! " He had tightened his hold of Ailean Sisealach's sleeve and was shaking it excitedly in an effort to compel him to understand. " You know Eachann Donn! " He drew closer and looked into Ailean's face and his voice pled. " You were there, little hero. Have pity on an old man and tell me now! "

Ailean Sisealach was in such distress that he did not know what to do or where to turn, the old man kept drawing his sleeve and looking in his face with a mixture of pleading and eagerness. In his vexation he suddenly began shouting at the old man in an angry voice. "There is nobody left in Srath Meadhonach, nobody at all! They are wiped out!" His face was red. He seemed to be trying to avert it and at the same time to keep his eye on his tormentor; and he tried to pull his sleeve away. "Nobody knows where they are!" he shouted, his voice rising. The old man was pulling his sleeve so strongly now that Ailean Sisealach staggered. He waved his free arm, getting shriller and more excited, "Do you understand? They are all gone . . . all . . . all!!"

The old man had been tightening his hold on the other's sleeve without knowing it, because of what was dawning on him. He now said in a small voice, very quietly, "Did you say—'all'?" Ailean Sisealach turned round on him a face of horror.

The old man released his hold and his hand fell to his side. He staggered and it looked as if he would have fallen. Then he stood swaying, turning this way and that a stricken face. He began to make a very strange gesture; he slowly raised both arms straight before him, the fists trembling. Letting one arm drop to his side he raised the other in the air, and after holding it a moment brought the fist down on his head. He began to beat himself on the head, gently, with his fist. Crying in a small, unnatural voice, "O—oh! God is punishing us for our sins! O—oh, my God!" Everyone stood helplessly, looking in dismay at the old man crying in a thin, wailing voice like a child and beating his fist against his head.

The dark, swarthy man had continued from the beginning to lean in a lazy attitude against the wall of the smithy, only watching everything out of the corners of his eyes in his impassive face. When the old man began crying out, his expression changed. He listened a moment, and suddenly startled them all by emitting a loud, angry noise like a snarl. The old man too turned his head and looked vaguely in the direction of the sudden noise.

"What sins have *you* committed, old man?" the swarthy man called to him rudely in his angry, snarling voice.

The old man was looking about in a bewildered manner; by his vague and wandering glance he quite clearly neither saw the other nor even connected the disturbance with himself, but was merely aware of some commotion gotten up near him. He turned to walk away, with a slow, hesitating step. The crowd drew back with alacrity and he passed through. The dark man shouted after him going, " Did you ever commit a sin in your life?"

He seemed possessed with a kind of anger of contempt. He unfolded his arms and took the pipe from his mouth. " ' Our sins,' says he. And, ' God is punishing us,' says he. Oh, for God's sake! " He spat on the ground. " A—ach the Black Factor! a thousand plagues on him and his shroud about him, and his share of Hell! "

The miller first recovered his sense of the situation. He took one glance round at the circle of faces and what he saw made him step forward. " Domhnall MacAmhlaidh! " he called out sternly, " I command you to keep silence! Is it not enough that such a thing has happened but you must be tempting God with curses?"

But the dark man was not abashed. He stood up from the wall and advanced his scowling face. " Is that you speaking up for the Black Foreigner, Miller? I would say it was more fitting that yourself should keep silence! "

The miller was somewhat taken aback by the accusation. " I am not speaking for the Black Foreigner," he said. " *You* know that, Domhnall Gorm. I am not the man. But there is such a thing as tempting God."

Domhnall Gorm was taken by a spasm of fury. He lifted his hand and dashed his pipe to the ground. " I am seven times tired of hearing that word," he shouted, livid. " Are you hearing, Miller? I am old tired of it. It's not God at all. It's just the same old black Satan, and his friend and servant the Black Foreigner. You're making a big song there about cursing, Miller, but it's my opinion God Himself has cursed the dog. What's wrong with cursing him then?" The dark man stood by the wall and cast a scowling, contemptuous glance around him. " Truly I look at you and I don't know what has got into the Gaidheil nowadays. It goes beyond me. Here is a pig of a Saxon at his old play of harrying. He gives

your roofs to the flames, turns your wives and your mothers
into the world houseless, and takes for himself the fields that
the forefathers brought back from the heather. And what do
you do? You sit on your arses and you can't think of anything but to make your eyes like cows' and lift up your hands
and say, ' God help us for we don't intend to help ourselves! '
Oh you have gone away from it altogether with godliness! "
he ended bitterly.

"And what now do *you* advise, Domhnall?"

"*Uh? What?* " The man started at hearing the voice close
to him. The walls of the smithy were thick, and the door
being at the inside of their thickness the smith leaning on its
lower portion had not been able to see the man standing close
to the wall outside. He had therefore come out, and stood at
the entrance. He was leaning his shoulder against the wall,
one hand stroking his beard while the other supported the
elbow, his blue eyes regarding the angry man with what
seemed an innocent look of enquiry.

Domhnall Gorm had been halted in his course, and he was
without the same fire of anger when he said, " There is only
one way with Saxons and invaders, Iain, and that is the way
of the ancestors—repel them. You are asking what I would
do to the Black Foreigner. He has rooted up and destroyed
our relatives and neighbours; then let us destroy him. When
he comes to harry us in like manner let the men of Gleann
Luachrach take him and them he has with him and tie them
together and throw them in the river, and let them end there.
Believe me, there is no man that will not say we did right."

The smith cast a hurried glance at the score or thereby of
men standing in a half-circle in front of his smithy. The
majority were still unrecovered from the shock of Ailean
Sisealach's news and the sight of the old man's helpless grief,
and Domhnall Gorm's outburst seemed to have affected them
only by increasing their alarm and confusion. Their faces
were strained and pale, full of fear or dismayed horror. Some
were staring fixedly at the ground before them, while the eyes
of others glanced about with a kind of helpless bewilderment.
But not so all. There were lips drawn back, fists clenched,

and lowering brows. For a single instant a look like concern passed through the smith's eyes, then at once he was looking at Domhnall Gorm with a mocking smile and a tilt of the head.

"So that's your way, Domhnall? Dirks, is it? Claymores out of the thatch, eh Domhnall?" The smith appeared to find something laughable there, for he threw back his head and let a gust of laughter from his great chest. There was something very strange about such laughter at such a time: a number turned their heads and looked blankly at him.

The smith addressed them. "I was sitting on Domhnall Gorm's roof," he said, seeming to try to control his amusement. "The time of the great wind two winters ago. Domhnall sent and I came and climbed up and sat on his roof to keep it from flying away. And the first thing I did was to sit down on some big hard thing that was there under the thatch. I put in my hand and when I had pulled several times with all my might out came the hilt. I put in my hand again and right enough there was the blade, three feet and half a foot of the good red rust. Believe me, men, it was such a weapon that I was in haste to put it back in its place for fear of doing a harm to myself, and I never told Domhnall Gorm I had found what he had laid bye yonder against the day!" He laughed. "No doubt but we will now see Great-Domhnall-of-the-Battles drawing the Red-Soft-One against the Foreigners!"

No one laughed with him. The miller and Domhnall Gorm, who were probably alone in having wholly understood what he was saying, showed only perplexity, the miller some concern and Domhnall Gorm blank amazement; without doubt he was only then hearing of the weapon in his thatch. For the rest, the smith might almost as well not have opened his mouth; only the sound of his laugh and his voice speaking had caused them to turn their faces towards him.

All at once a man in the crowd broke into a frenzied shouting, throwing both his hands above his head. "God's curse on him! God's curse on him! God's curse on him!" As if it broke the spell that held them, shouts and cries were suddenly raised in all directions. The smith too was suddenly shouting and no longer pretending amusement. He was shouting to command silence. But the angry voices continued among the crowd. " Curse the tyrant! " " Destroy the foreign dog! " " To the river with him! " The smith had stepped forward from his door and was shouting at the top of his voice, his face concerned. " Listen, men! You don't know what you're saying! Listen to me! "

At last they became quiet.

" Listen, men! What you are wanting is impossible. Be calm and consider the matter reasonably. Suppose we did that thing, suppose we took it into our own hands to defend ourselves and to avenge our relatives and neighbours. What would happen then? You were at Dùn Eachainn. You saw the cannons and the red soldiers with their muskets. It was only Maighstir Sachairi that saved us all from being murdered that day. Remember those we have to do with now are not accustomed to stop at killing women and weaponless men. If it was only the Black Factor what you are wanting us to do would be easy enough, whether it would be right or not. But if we did that thing, if we killed the Black Foreigner or drowned him in the river, would that be the end of him? would the matter be let rest there? Believe me it would only be the beginning. The power is in their hands now and they will not be slow to use it without fear or conscience, for there is none to call them to account. The red soldiers would be let loose amongst us. These are beasts. You have heard from the grandfathers how they murder even children and old men. And we are defenceless. Men, if the Factor has his way with us the roofs will be burned over our heads and we will be made into beggars and landless, without a stick or a sod to call our own. That is bad enough surely, and may God keep it far from us! But let you lay a finger on the Factor and we will all be murdered as well, for yon English know no pity when the day is with them. Believe me what has happened in Srath Meadhonach is a small and trivial thing to what would happen in Gleann Luachrach then."

A voice: " God help the Gaidheil now, in the power of the Saxons! "

"In the power of the Saxons we are. And therefore and because there is no help for it we can only conduct ourselves like men that hold their lives and possessions at the mercy of their enemies and the enemies of their race. At one time it was different altogether. It was not a safe thing in those days for an enemy to show his face here or to cast his eye upon these glens. The first man that he met would be Mac 'Ic Eachainn,* and five hundred broadswords at his back. And so it was for a thousand years. But it is on us the two days have come. Mac 'Ic Eachainn is now no better than an Englishman. He does not speak our language. We are nothing to him, no better than foreigners. He is even in this himself, so it is said. Men, our enemies are too strong for us, for behind the Black Factor is Mac 'Ic Eachainn, and behind him is the Parliament of England. Domhnall Gorm can speak about destroying the Black Foreigner, but that is only Domhnall Gorm's swagger. Remember he has the Law with him, the English law, and there is no justice in it for the Gaidheil. As far as I can see, men, we are in such a case just now that nothing can save us unless it be a miracle of God; and how can we hope He will deliver us if He hears us using swelling words and threatening to take vengeance into our own hands? Truly men there is no safety and no escape unless we keep quiet. We must speak soft and keep quiet, and that's my word to you."

"Well argued out, Smith! You have the gift! It's easy to see who are the elders here! One would say it was Maighstir Sachairi speaking, you have his words and the sound of him so well!" Domhnall Gorm spoke bitingly. "Smith! it's a minister lost you are!"

He took a slow look round at the men, who had been impressed and reduced to silence, and his lip curled.

"So we are to keep quiet and speak soft! We are not to defend ourselves!" He suddenly became furious again, waved his hand in the air. "When they burn the roofs over our heads we are to stand by and give them leave! When they

* Patronymic of the Chief.

drive us like cattle, we are to thank them and shake them by
the hand! And what about Srath Meadhonach and Gleann
Mór—is the like of that to be let pass? Was I understanding
you, Smith?—the whole of a countryside is to be unpeopled
at the whim of one bad man and nobody is to call him to
account—is that what you are asking of us?"

The smith looked stern and angry. "You heard what I was
saying, Domhnall. Nobody is to raise his hand against the
Factor or even to be heard speaking against him. The safety
of every person in Gleann Luachrach depends on it."

The dark man only became angrier. "It's you were speaking about safety, Smith! *I* was saying a devilish wrong had
been done in Srath Meadhonach by that son of Satan the
Black Foreigner. And if there is a small grain of manhood in
us it is for us to avenge it on him. A—ach! do you know
what it is, all this? Only fear." He snapped his fingers.
"Smith! you can speak soft in your own smithy reek!"

The smith was holding his fists clenched by his sides, with
an effort restraining his anger. "Domhnall! you are bolder
to-day than I have seen you!"

They stood glaring at each other; it almost looked as if at
any moment they might fly at each other's throats.

The miller had said nothing all this time. When Domhnall
Gorm was shouting and lifting his fist he kept his eyes on him
with a stern expression. He watched the smith gravely, looking
from him to the others, listening to him. When Domhnall
Gorm began a second time he drew his brows together.
At this point, as if he judged the time had come when he
must interfere, he stepped forward and addressed him.

"Domhnall Gorm! that will do now. The smith has told
you already it's nonsense you're speaking and why the thing
you're wanting is impossible. You are only putting us all in
greater danger, for if your words come to the Factor's ears
he will say we need keeping in order and that will give him
his excuse."

Domhnall Gorm was to reply. "Another elder . . . ?" he
began. But the miller waved it aside with a massive, dusty
arm. "That will do now, Domhnall! You force me to ask

whether you think you are such a man that all Gleann Luachrach should be put in danger only for your sake. We know
you, Domhnall. You are a man given to words. When you
begin you go on, until you don't know yourself what you are
saying. You were always a noisy fellow, Domhnall, a blus-
terer. Now keep silence a little. I have something to say
myself."

He looked round slowly.

"Men, listen to me. There is one thing every one of you
seems to have forgotten. You were all present yon day when
the Black Foreigner got us to Dùn Eachainn to murder us.
You saw what took place that time. You know we might all
be dead to-day if it were not for Maighstir Sachairi? Well,
men, I think we are not doing right if we let fear take hold
of us just now. It is true we are in great danger. You heard
Ailean Sisealach when he told you how the people of Gleann
Mór and Srath Meadhonach are wiped out, and we know too
well that the Black Foreigner would do the same to us if he
could. But if we are in danger we should not be without hope;
we should remember that we are not without a protector. For
if Maighstir Sachairi saved us that day at Dùn Eachainn, why
would he not be protecting us now? Why would he be protecting us at one time and deserting us at another time?"

The miller's glance happened to fall on Domhnall Gorm,
and he stopped and looked at him. "I see your face, Domhnall
Gorm, and I know what you would be saying. You are saying,
If Maighstir Sachairi is protecting us, why did he let the
Factor burn the pasture then? Men, don't listen to Domhnall
Gorm! Maighstir Sachairi is a man to keep his own counsel
and he has not told any of us why he did that. But if he let
the Black Foreigner burn the pasture he had his reason, and
the reason was not that he had given way before the Factor
or that he could not protect us any longer. We know that
because he told us to sow the seed. For it would not be
reasonable to think that he told us to sow not expecting that
in due course we should reap.

"Consider, men, the kind of man that Maighstir Sachairi
is. When he came to Gleann Luachrach many thought he

was a hard man. At that time there was a great deal of foolishness and vanity, more than was fitting. Maighstir Sachairi was against it, and he did not spare us. Maybe he was hard, but if he was, it was for our sakes and to keep us from sin. But what nobody can ever say is that he was not *just*. Maighstir Sachairi was never one thing to one man and another thing to another. He has lived among us for twenty years, everybody was bound to know his words and actions, and nobody ever heard one unjust thing that he has said or done.

" And that is not all either. When Maighstir Sachairi came to Gleann Luachrach there were many Domhnall Gorms in it, and some that were not only talkers and users of words like Domhnall Gorm but were strong men and very determined on their own way, and they were against Maighstir Sachairi when he would have us give over our foolishness and vain amusements. But Maighstir Sachairi was alone and he was stronger than all, he made even Fearchar the Poet yield to him at last."

The miller looked round the company; then leaned a little forward and raised his hand.

" What if the Factor would like to harm us? He is only a man. And if there are others with him, they also are only men. Maighstir Sachairi is stronger than all of them. Maighstir Sachairi is a strong man, even the Factor is afraid of him. And he is a just man, he will not be silent when things are done that are against justice. More than that, he is a man of God, Maighstir Sachairi, a man of prayer, and therefore God will be with him in the things he does. Trust to Maighstir Sachairi, men. He is for us. Let there be no more speaking about violence and revenging ourselves on the Black Foreigner; it is God that will punish him. And let us not be afraid either. Maighstir Sachairi is standing between us and harm. He is our minister, put over us by God to be our guide and protector. He will not let us be swallowed up. Only let us leave the matter in his hands, and if it is God's will nothing will happen to us.

" Men, this is what I say; and if you are wise, you will let it be the last word—Leave it to the minister. *Put your hope in Maighstir Sachairi!"*

There was a chorus of assent. "You are right, Miller!" "That is the truest word yet!" "That's good advice now!"

One small man in the front of the crowd was turning about, looking first over one shoulder and then over the other at the men about him, shouting excitedly, "Maighstir Sachairi will save us!" "Maighstir Sachairi is a great man, a strong man," he shouted, "Maighstir Sachairi is the strongest man in Alba!" He raised one arm and held it up before him in the air. Then with the other hand he made a sharp cutting movement, downward, past the wrist. "I would cut off my hand for him!"

The voices in the crowd continued, expressing agreement with the miller and the excited man.

"True for you, Uilleam Beag!" "Maighstir Sachairi is afraid of no man living!" "We have only to trust to Maighstir Sachairi!" "Maighstir Sachairi is only waiting, he knows what he will do!"

CHAPTER SIX

M AIGHSTIR SACHAIRI paced to and fro, to and fro. Now
and then he paused and listened. He could hear their
voices from here. When they called out orders to each other
he could distinguish words and phrases. " No, no! not that
way! Here, under her neck! Ready? Now then, *pull!*" At
last he approached the window with a hesitating step and
looked cautiously, standing back a little as if afraid or un-
willing to be seen.

The cow was still lying on her side. They had that minute
failed again to raise her and given up the attempt. They were
standing round looking down at her, the ropes and the pieces
of wood still in their hands. In a little one man turned and
said something to his neighbour who without looking up
shook his head with a doubtful movement. Two or three
others raised their heads and looked across at the first man
and one of them must have addressed him for he turned
towards him and Maighstir Sachairi could see his lips moving
in reply. Then another stepped across and stood behind the
animal's neck, pointing with his hand. He bent down and
squatted on his heels, describing some motion with his hands
and looking up from one to the other. Several leant forward
together, speaking and pointing. Maighstir Sachairi could
hear a low sound of their voices. The cow lay with her back
towards him. From where he stood he could see the emaciated
creature's bones sticking up so sharply that it seemed they
must come through the shrunken skin. She lay quite motionless at the feet of the group, her head on the ground, her
neck stretched out. But shortly she moved; a tremor passed
through her, she kicked out with her legs and with a spas-
modic, heaving movement made as if to rise. Some of the

men jumped clear of her legs; others rushed in behind her and pushed and lifted, helping her. She reached her knees. They closed in round her, pushing and shouting, " *Now* she'll do it! Up with her! " But just as it seemed a final heave would have brought her to her feet 'her hindquarters sank again. They pushed the harder, calling, " She'll do it yet! Push now! " But it was the cow's last effort. She turned her head once towards them, rolling her straining eyes, then fell back on her side. She stretched out her neck along the ground and a lowing noise like a long groan came from her mouth. A man standing by her head bent and looked at her, and straightening himself lifted his arms and let them fall limp to his sides.

Just then all turned their heads and looked up the glen. Maighstir Sachairi was to cross to the other side of the window so that he could see what they were looking at, but he remembered he would expose himself to the view of any that happened to look up and not wishing to be seen remained where he was. The men continued to stand looking up the glen. A barking of dogs was heard in that direction. The noise came nearer. After a little a few more cattle came slowly into view, two men driving them and some boys with them with sticks in their hands. When they came to where the cow was lying, the two men went over and looked down at her. They spoke to the others and turned to consider her again, their hands on their hips. The cattle stood still where they stopped driving them, one or two turned their heads slowly from side to side in search of something they could eat or lowering their heads blew long breaths on the dusty ground. The men and boys that had been driving them had for the moment turned their attention to the cow. All at once some-one called out in a sharp, warning tone. All wheeled round. Now one of the other cattle was in the act of lying down. They rushed across and began shouting, pushing the animal, striking it with sticks. But to no purpose; it lay down and in spite of their utmost efforts lay still and refused to be roused. One of the men started to shout and gesticulate, pointing to the cattle that were still on their feet. The other ran and the

boys with him to drive them off. After considerable noise, the
boys shouting, dogs barking, the cattle moved away slowly,
urged on by cries and blows. All stood and watched their
slow, unsteady progress. After a little the first man put his
hand up to his mouth and called out to the other who was
driving the cattle, " Keep them moving! "

Maighstir Sachairi turned from the window and went and
sat in his chair. He put his fingers to his brow and leant back.
When he had sat for a time, his eyes closed, a groan escaped
him. He was thinking—and it was not for the first time that
day—that more he could not bear. He could not be a witness
of such things and stand passive. He could not. It was not in
his nature. If they were to be, he must actively suffer them,
he must suffer with his people, the same loss as they suffered.
Or he must be able to comfort them, to exhort them to
patience, holding before them the meaning of their suffering.
But when he could do neither—not knowing whence was their
suffering, or if it *had* any meaning, not knowing indeed that
they did not suffer through his fault—then he could neither
suffer nor find relief from suffering, and it was unbearable.
Maighstir Sachairi drew his fingers wearily along his brow,
then resting his elbow on the chair arm, laid his cheek against
his hand. He closed his eyes—and was so startled by the
vividness with which a scene leapt immediately in front of
his mind that he hastily opened them again and glanced round
nervously; as if to reassure himself by the look of familiar
things.

What had leapt before him, startled him, was what he had
been witness of that morning . . . Maighstir Sachairi was
always one to be up betimes: but of late his thoughts had
been such as to drive sleep from his eyelids; his mind worked
so, considering this and that, that he had come almost to
dread the night; and it was with relief that he rose from his
bed with the first glimmer of dawn. That morning too he got
up with the light and coming into his study sat down near the
window and began as usual to read the daily portion. It
happened that in the methodical course he was used to take
year by year through Holy Writ he had reached the book of

Revelation, and to that day's portion there fell the sixth chapter. Reading, he came to the place where it says: " *And, lo, there was a great earthquake; and the sun became black as sackcloth of hair, and the moon became as blood; and the stars of heaven fell unto the earth, even as a fig tree casteth her untimely figs, when she is shaken of a mighty wind. And the heaven departed as a scroll when it is rolled together; and every mountain and island were moved out of their places. And the kings of the earth, and the great men, and the rich men, and the chief captains, and the mighty men, and every bondman, and every free man, hid themselves in the dens and in the rocks of the mountains; and said to the mountains and rocks, Fall on us and hide us from the face of him that sitteth on the throne, and from the wrath of the Lamb: For the great day of his wrath is come; and who shall be able to stand?"*

The day of his wrath is come; and who shall be able to stand? Maighstir Sachairi could not tell why at that point he should have experienced such a spasm of fear as used to overcome him in his childhood and unregenerate youth at the thought of the day of the wrath of God. Putting down the Bible, he rose hastily in some alarm and stood at the window.

The breadth of Gleann Luachrach lay before him southwards, coming to its solid shapes through the thin haze the sun was dispersing, rising at that moment above the hills to the east. Maighstir Sachairi noticed with some surprise that smoke was pouring from almost every roof and chimney within sight. It was unusual for every fire in the glen to be kindled before dawn, and he wondered in his mind what could explain the circumstance. Evidently all were in full preparation for something that was to take place that day, but in the stress of his troubled thoughts he had been—he only now realised how far—removed from the daily concerns of the people—even, for days at a time, from speech with them—and he had not heard what was afoot. Or maybe he had heard and had forgotten . . . But happening to raise his eyes towards the upper portions of the glen, he saw what the matter was.

As he had foreseen, and as the Factor intended, the burning of the heath pasture had had ruinous results for the

people. At the best of times their heavy stock of cattle depended much in spring upon the grass among the heather.
But as misfortune would have it, they were compelled that
spring to be almost entirely dependent upon it, for other
fodder had never been less plentiful. When it was burned, the
numerous cattle in the entire glen were left without subsis-
tence, and in consequence they starved. For weeks they were
to be seen, whole herds together, wandering about in search
of food. They ranged the blackened hillsides, finding every
place where the green points were reappearing. There were
frequently crowds of them along the river where they were
chewing the weeds that grew in stagnant eddies. In the end
they had eaten up everything within reach, even the moss
from the stones. The people were compelled to watch their
cattle wandering about in famished droves, and those of them
that had houses or out-buildings that stood on declivities
were frequently obliged to post children armed with sticks or
keep watch themselves to prevent the starving beasts from
tearing down and attempting to eat the thatch. What Maighstir Sachairi saw when he looked up the glen was a herd of
the cattle approaching, driven on by men and dogs, and he at
once understood what was afoot and why the glenspeople
had risen that day before the dawn. There must be a sale of
cattle in the Machair, and they were sending there most of
the animals that remained alive. Maighstir Sachairi looked at
the approaching drove, and at the sight he could have grat.
At the same time, too, he felt revolted by something about it
that seemed grisly, horrible, and unnatural. The cattle were
so emaciated that many of them resembled skeletons. They
walked only at a snail's pace, moving their legs slowly and
with difficulty, and as they staggered along their heads
drooped and lolled about, the eyes without life staring dully.
Only the dogs constantly barking at their heels kept them on
the move. He looked at the men; there seemed to be no conversation going on among them; they walked for the most
part singly, wrapped in their plaids, their faces impassive. All
trailed past below his window in weird, almost ghostly procession, all, except only the dogs, silent. They had no sooner

passed than others appeared. And so it had been all morning; since the breaking of day until now one procession of starving cattle after another staggering past below his window . . .

This was the vision of emaciated beasts that had leapt before Maighstir Sachairi's mind with such startling vividness, and caused him to open his eyes hastily. He now closed his eyes again and leant back in his chair. He began to think of his people, the men with the cattle, of their patience and resigned faces, and his bowels yearned for them. They were not hoping to get prices for such animals—everyone knew the cattle stock, their chief wealth, was a complete loss—they were only hoping to save what they could from the ruin of their livelihood and avoid the wholesale slaughter of their own beasts that was the only alternative. Yet he had heard no word of complaint from any of them, nor seen any sign that they were not prepared to accept with an equal resignation whatever might be in store, even if it was such a calamity as had befallen the people of Gleann Mór and Srath Meadhonach.

It was this their patient and meek spirit that made his chiefest torment. A dignity and resignation in their faces struck him, cut him like a mute reproach. Often, when he was alone, or in the night, their eyes appeared before him—not the eyes of any one, but many; or it was as if all looked at him in two, impersonal, eyes—and their expression seemed to say to him, Why are you doing this to us? Maighstir Sachairi remembered again with feelings of shame the day a number had come to him. They came with diffidence and hesitation, fearful lest they should be at fault in coming. Taking off their bonnets, they stood shyly. Each man, he saw, had put on his best clothes. The miller spoke for them, in a respectful voice, an apologetic smile on his broad, honest face: They had been sent by the rest of the people to ask the minister for his advice on a small matter of their own, if it was his pleasure to give them an answer. They knew that Maighstir Sachairi had his own opinion about certain things and that he would communicate it to them when he judged it good they should know, and they asked him to believe they were not so presumptuous as to wish to hurry him. But there was a small matter in which his advice would greatly help them if he could without inconvenience give it. As he knew, it was now the time of sowing; indeed it was perhaps a little past it. But a beginning had not been made to the work because many of the people said it was no use to do so, as it was likely they would not be having a harvest that year. They were not presuming to ask him about that, since he had not himself seen fit to tell them. But they would be greatly under obligation to him if he would simply say, in one word, what was his advice, whether they should sow or not. Maighstir Sachairi had looked at them, the miller and six or seven others, respectable well-doing men, honest, upright persons whom he had never known in a grave fault—and suddenly turning away he went and stood at the window, his back to them. He was aware that by acting so he might cause them to think they had done wrong in coming to him, that he was angry with them; but he could not help it. The truth was he could not face them. Their respectful looks, their eyes, reproached him. When he looked at their faces, honest and kindly, so familiar, he became filled with such emotions of pity and sorrow that he feared to lose control and weep before them. With his back to them, he was still aware of them standing humbly there, and struggled to master himself and give them an answer. But what answer? Should he let his pity speak, and say what would reassure them? He knew they would take such an answer as a sign and promise that he was going to protect them, and all their hearts would be lightened. But what if God should reveal His will at last, and it should be His purpose to scourge and punish them? What then?—he would merely have made the judgment a hundred-fold more heavy to endure, adding to their sorrow the bitterness of new hopes lately shattered. For that he turned again to pitying them. He thought of all the rest and the feelings with which they must be awaiting the answer he would give—everything they possessed or knew, all their hopes, their whole lives depended on it. He was aware with pain of those seven or eight standing behind him, of their humility and patience and their readiness to resume the burden of anxiety should he only say that it inconvenienced him to give an answer. Nor could he be insensible of their delicacy in the manner of approaching him, their consideration of him rather than of themselves, and that even when the matter concerned their very lives. He had often in the past had occasion to reprove them sternly for small shortcomings, but at that moment he could only find them admirable. Of a sudden pity swelled in his throat and his eyes, and almost before he knew it he had called out in a gruff voice the one word, " Sow! " He heard their murmured thanks. When after a little he turned round from the window, all had gone silently out of the room.—And suddenly he was feeling that what he had done was not what he ought to have done, that he had misled them, and wronged them therefore . . . Sitting there, his eyes closed, Maighstir Sachairi experienced that moment over again.

And again he could not understand this feeling that he had wronged the people. His pain and trouble was that he could no longer understand anything, things or himself. Himself least of all. Something had happened to him—so much he knew. But what it was and what had caused it, that he could not discover, that he found more incomprehensible the more he pondered it. For thirty years there had never been a moment when he did not see his duty. Indeed he had never conceived it possible that his duty could be obscure. That it should at times be hard to perform, he could understand; he had often found it so. But not obscure, never obscure. How should a man's duty be obscure? With God's Word before him it ought to be clear enough, though often difficult, often against his human judgment and the current of his desires. He had been such a man that he had never doubted where his duty lay, and because he had no other will than to perform it he had been strong and fearless, able to overcome. And now—how to explain it?—something had happened to him. On the gravest occasion of his whole life and ministry his duty had suddenly become dark before him, he no longer knew his way, all at once his power to act was inhibited at the source, for he saw the end of every course of action so strangely that it looked at the same time like his duty and a sin. A wicked tyrant, trusting in his own power and the backing of a distant and unjust Law, threatened to let loose upon his people such horrors as scarcely accompanied the course of cruel war—or so it seemed; and he their minister and protector, he who had never feared the face of powers and tyrants, sat in a kind of paralysis of nerve and will, fearful lest a human oppression should hide the form of divine justice and in opposing it he should be at fault, not discerning the Hand of God. He could understand that a proud and wicked man like the Black Factor might be chosen and allowed by God to be the instrument of His correction, even as in olden times God's elect people had for their sins been delivered up to scourging at the hands of heathen princes. But why could he not see whether this was such a case? Why had perception deserted him? and with it the power of action? Why was he so soon become weak? Sometimes in this night of doubt he almost longed to see the Factor, as if he felt that at sight of him his duty might somehow become clear again; longed for some act or external thing, so that he might perchance find certainty in looking outward, since within were only doubts and darkness . . . Maighstir Sachairi groaned again. Truly he could not recognise himself any longer. Less than an hour before, standing by the window, he had noticed a man turn his head in his direction. And although this happened quite by chance, and he knew he could not be seen, yet he obeyed the impulse to draw back into the room and hide himself. Why had he done that? Why was he ashamed and guilty before the people? Had he wronged them? Maighstir Sachairi leant forward, chin on hand, and pondered that thought a long time.

He saw that the change had begun with the discovery of Mairi-of-Eoghann-Gasda's sin, and his conversation with her. And he understood how a thing so shocking, followed as it had been by such a vision of sin in his own mind, could have shaken his confidence and put it into his thoughts that there might be other possibilities than those he had only considered hitherto; possibilities which became certainties later that day

when for some reason the conviction took hold of him that
God was in this. What he could not understand was why that
conviction also had left him. Had it been an error of his
human judgment? And if so why when it left him did he not
return to his former certainty, that the Factor was the agent
only of human wickedness and a Devil's servant? In which
conviction had his judgment been at fault? What had become
of the assurance that had never formerly deserted him? Why
were there only warring possibilities in his mind, whose ceaseless strife destroyed his peace?

Maighstir Sachairi propped both his elbows on his knees
and bent his face into his hands. If only there were no more
than uncertainty! he thought. What was this feeling that had
come to torture him, this obscure sense as of *guilt?* What had
he done? He could not tell, but he knew that since he lost
his first conviction and assurance it had been there, gnawing
his mind. Even as he sat with Mairi-of-Eoghann-Gasda he
had begun to feel guilty, he did not know of what. While he
spoke to the Factor, looking at the men starting fires along
the hillside, he had felt vaguely uneasy, as if he were at fault.
And since then it had grown with his uncertainty, nourished
apparently upon his doubts. He felt he should be up and
doing in this crisis, every moment of the day and night he felt
it, that there was something he should be *doing*—but what?
—and so long as he did not act he felt guilty, of something,
towards someone. When he considered his people he felt it
was towards them he was guilty, that he had wronged them
somewhere. When he thought of God it was against Him he
felt he had offended. At that thought Maighstir Sachairi
groaned; this feeling also was something he did not understand. It occurred to him that formerly when he encountered
dangers and difficulties it had always been his practice to lay
the matter before God in his prayers, and thus he had ob-
tained both relief and guidance. And that he had done on this
occasion also, constantly with many sighs and groans. But
this time there had been no enlightenment, nor help nor
cheering.

For it seemed to him too that since he began to be troubled

God had removed far from him. In what he had offended against His justice, even against His forbearance and clemency, he could not tell. But all those weeks he had been deprived of the sense of His presence. And it was terrible. In his distress, in his doubts and hesitations, his struggle and striving, in his ceaseless pondering and reasoning this way and that, in the weariness that began to grow upon him—to feel that he was alone, that God had left him . . .

After a little, Maighstir Sachairi raised his head. For a long time he sat motionless looking into the hearth, his eyes full of a look of pain and suffering.

All at once he was on his feet, startled. Across his thoughts, in which he had been withdrawn so far as to the contemplation of eternal things, there had shattered a sudden, loud reverberation. He stood blinking confusedly, unable to come to himself. After a while, suddenly, it came again, filling the room; the sharp, cracking report of a gun. Alarmed, Maighstir Sachairi hurried to the window, for the shot seemed to have been fired close outside.

With one glance he saw what it was.

He had forgotten about the cattle that were too weak with hunger to rise from the ground. The men were stooping and examining them, one man holding a gun.

2

For some reason Maighstir Sachairi remembered at that moment about Bean na h-Airde Móire. A message had come for him the previous day to go to the old woman because she was taken sick, and they thought she might die; but the thing had instantly gone out of his mind. Surprised by this new and most reprehensible forgetfulness he hurried out at once. "Lachlan!" he called out, emerging into the open air.

The head of Lachlan MacMhuirich appeared round the stable door, and was at once withdrawn. Shortly the door was pulled wide open and he reappeared, leading the horse. He held the bridle while Maighstir Sachairi mounted, and Maighstir Sachairi was conscious of his eye fixed upon him.

But he kept his own eyes averted and without again addressing him touched the horse into motion and at once rode off.

Riding slowly he fell again at once to pondering. He wished he had the certainty that Lachlan MacMhuirich seemed to have, wherever he had found it. The man had been in Gleann Mór and Srath Meadhonach when the day was with the Factor there. He had been a witness of it all. More, he had already suffered in his person some of the results of what had been done; for being hurt and benighted and needing food and shelter he had found none to minister to his necessities where formerly had been many, and had known pain, hunger and exposure for a day and two nights in a smoking wilderness where instead and in other days he would have found warmth and food and human hands. He had thus every reason for seeing the matter under the aspect of a senseless barbarity, for so he had experienced it. Instead, the gloomy fellow had surprised, and if it must be admitted disturbed, him by bearing no grudge against those whose act had caused his pain, by seeing in it a human oppression not at all, but the Hand of God. Since he began to recover his strength he had not ceased (and even seemed to seek opportunities) to assail his uncertainty with his own assurance. " This was from God, Maighstir Sachairi! There is no doubt but this is the judgment of God! "

The judgment of God—the judgment of God—Maighstir Sachairi could hear him. Recently there had been times when his senses seemed to have become sharpened to a point of almost unbearable acuteness, so that whatever he felt or saw—and above all whatever he *heard*—he experienced with a sharpness and an intimacy that were startling, often even to the verge of pain. It was so now. He heard the voice of Lachlan MacMhuirich close in his ear. It was repeating the favourite phrase, and in spite of his desire not to hear it it went on repeating it, faster and faster. Then it changed and began to say it slowly, very slowly, exaggerating to the point of the fantastic a certain characteristic note of something like servility. The judgment of God—The judgment of God. . . .

Maighstir Sachairi made an effort of taking control of
of himself. He gave a little shrug of his shoulder. Despite
his unfailing performance of his duties, and his theological
soundness—perhaps indeed because of a too great readiness
of his in the expression of right opinions—he had never
been able to rid himself quite of the last vague doubts of
Lachlan MacMhuirich's straightforwardness. It was a very
vague and undefined feeling that he had about him. The
man had never given him any reason for distrust; externally,
in his conduct, he appeared faultless, not having given in
ten years the least cause for blame. Yet the feeling remained.
Perhaps (Maighstir Sachairi had told himself) he misunder-
stood this feeling. Maybe it was not mistrust at all but only
dislike; an obscure revulsion inspired by the man's unpre-
possessing appearance, the dead whiteness of his skin, his
blind white eye gleaming damply, the other by contrast looking unnaturally bright and inquisitive. As if a hen put her
head on one side! Whatever it was, he had about Lachlan
MacMhuirich some obscure doubt or hesitation. And perhaps it had been in consequence of this that he no sooner
began to speak with his tone of confidence about " the judgment of God " than Maighstir Sachairi was immediately
swayed in his mind towards the contrary opinion. In solitude
and in his secret mind the thought that God had judged the
people came, terrible, and stood before him with a silent
clarity, bearing the solid aspect of a truth: but when he
heard his own thought spoken, and from Lachlan Mac-
Mhuirich's lips, all at once the idea appeared before him
lacking that body of probability, looking thin and arbitrary,
and something in him was moved to opposition and denial.
Lachlan MacMhuirich had only to start again with his
mournful recitation; long before he got the length of " This
was from God, Maighstir Sachairi! " Maighstir Sachairi was
saying to himself, " Not at all! " or, " Very unlikely! " or,
simply, " Perhaps! "* Latterly the mere appearance of
Lachlan MacMhuirich was enough to put him in a frame of

---

*Ma's fhior, literally, If it is true! An expression of strong incredulity.

mind to see the whole thing as a simple act of tyranny.

And now, only from thinking of him, he began as he rode along to touch the edge of such a mood. He began to reflect, with a kind of spiteful anger that was most unlike him, that they were a strangely unlikely folk who claimed to have received the grace to discern God's Purpose. He was thinking of the occasion when he went at their request to interview his brethren. It was just after the Black Factor had first made the suggestion to him that the glen might be improved by being unpeopled, and he had repudiated it with indignation. He went to see his brethren, finding them both together in the house of Maighstir Tormod in Srath Meadhonach, and it was then they told him that the Factor and Mac 'Ic Eachainn were determined on expelling all the people from the glens and that they saw in this the hand of God in judgment. He had sat for a long time in silence, his head bowed, for it distressed him deeply to think what they must be suffering seeing the matter in that light· and he was trying to see what it was necessary or possible to say in order to help them. At last he raised his eyes and was to speak. But he did not speak. Maighstir Tormod was glooming about, too obviously avoiding his eye; an embarrassed but sulkily defiant look on his long sallow face. Maighstir Iain when he, next, turned to him, broke into a grin of most unmeasured width and drummed with his fingers on the tops of his plump knees, grinning at him;—he had had no reason to redden like a lobster merely because he was surprised taking a cautious sideways look. . . . Maighstir Sachairi had got to his feet and without saying a word strode straight out of the room and returned home. He was thinking of that occasion now. "Two farms added to the farm of each of them!" he said, unaware that he was speaking aloud, "their pasturage enclosed at the charge of Mac 'Ic Eachainn—new roads to be made only for their convenience—and a new manse built for Tormod—*Fich*! What do we know of ministers who take gifts from Satan for serving God!" He gave an angry shrug of his shoulders and raising his head began looking about him.

The sun had some time fully risen above the hills behind him and dispelled the mists of morning. It was full Spring. The air was very warm, almost without movement, yet with a faint refreshing coolness when it touched the cheek—as if a single icicle had melted each moment in the centre of the heavens. Everywhere the fields were greening over with the springing corn. The trees were clad. As he rode past he could see many large dewdrops gleaming where they had gathered in scarcely opened leaves. One would have thought that not every bush only but every twig had its bird. The Spring was everywhere. It seemed to Maighstir Sachairi the whole glen resounded with it. He looked up at the blue, morning sky. He looked at the farms and crofts dotted along the slopes among trees. The lark got up from his horse's feet, up, straight into the blue, bursting its throat. . . .

All at once Maighstir Sachairi's whole being was filled with indignation, he felt himself swept by a fire of anger. He raised his fist. " This is just *you*, Mr. Byars! "—again he was speaking aloud. " But wait you, Tyrant! "

At a little distance down the slope the house of the mill stood near the river bank. The miller himself was standing at the window, and every now and then speaking over his shoulder into the room behind him. " He has stopped now! " " No, he is still standing there, he seems to be uncertain. . . " " I wonder. . . " And then, " He is coming here! " He took off his bonnet and hurried out, a look of concern breaking through on his grave, rather impassive face, and was at the door as Maighstir Sachairi rode up at a canter.

" Good day to you, Maighstir Sachairi! "

" Good day to *you*, Miller! " called out Maighstir Sachairi in a loud hearty voice.

The miller called over his shoulder, " Eachann! come here and take Maighstir Sachairi's horse! " Then he came forward and held the bridle for the minister to dismount.

" Have you had your meal yet, Maighstir Sachairi? "

" I don't believe I have yet," said Maighstir Sachairi, stepping to the ground.

"Then you come just in time, Maighstir Sachairi. You will take it with us."

Since hearing the minister's hearty tone the miller wore a quietly pleased and satisfied look. He gave the reins to the lad who had emerged from the house and stood back to let Maighstir Sachairi enter before him.

Maighstir Sachairi went into the room the miller calling out at his back, "Wife! here is Maighstir Sachairi come to take his meal with us!"

The woman turned round and curtseyed, darting a half-frightened glance at the minister. The old man the miller's father, was sitting in his chair. He looked round when the minister came in, and putting up a slow hand that shook a little took the bonnet from his white head and held it on his knees. "You are honouring us," he said in his quavering voice. The small children had at once got off their chairs by the table and were standing shyly, looking at their feet, awed by the presence.

"Good day to you, Gilleasbuig! and to you Peigi Dhonn!" said Maighstir Sachairi in the room, patting a curly head. "God's blessing on the house!"

"May God bless yourself, Maighstir Sachairi!"

The small boy whose head had been patted by the minister was standing still, too awed to move, clutching in his fist the horn spoon he had been preparing to use to his meal. The miller, who had the grave kindness of a big, stern man towards children, bent down to him and took him by the arm. "Here now, Gilleasbuig Beag, come away from the chair and let Maighstir Sachairi be sitting down. Go you, little mannikin, and stand beside Sine."

Maighstir Sachairi smiled, watching the boy go shyly and stand beside his sister. "So this is Benjamin is it, Miller?"

The miller and his wife laughed a little at that, finding the minister so genial. "If so then I am Isaac, it seems," said the old man Gilleasbuig Liath following the minister's humour, his voice quavering more than ever when he smiled.

The miller now poured whisky into a glass and gave it to the minister, saying, "Do us the honour, Maighstir Sachairi!"

He filled one for Gilleasbuigh Liath and another for himself. The minister took off his bonnet; all excepting only Gilleasbuig Liath stood with heads bowed reverently for the blessing.

There was an uncomfortable moment when after they were sat down the wife pushed the jug to Maighstir Sachairi. The miller caught her agitated glances in his direction and noticing what she was doing looked down at his hands and sat, his face reddening. Gilleasbuig Liath may have noticed too for he coughed loosely and turned his head away. Maighstir Sachairi observing nothing of this had taken the jug absently and from habit and had already tilted it up when he noticed the little of watery stuff that was in it, and stopped. The woman's voice was small, apologetic. "It's poor milk the cows are giving just now." She was not looking, but keeping her eyes in a frightened way on her husband.

Maighstir Sachairi recovered himself at once. He pushed the jug back. "That is so, wife," he said as if there had been nothing unusual in the circumstance—as if it might have resulted for instance from the season of the year. "But give the milk to the children. For us that are grown-up here is something better." And so saying he took and poured the whisky over the porridge and immediately began to ply his spoon and to eat with appetite. They began to eat also, the children absorbedly and wholeheartedly, with a children's appetite. But the miller and his wife were silent and constrained because of what had almost been mentioned.

Maighstir Sachairi did not appear to notice it. Eating heartily he raised his eyes after a little and looking round let them rest on the woman. Under the white currachd appeared along her brow her hair, dark brown and abundant. Her eyelids she kept lowered and a wrinkle in her brow—a still bonny face, looking demure and troubled. A faint reminiscent smile came along the minister's lips. Gilleasbuig Liath's shaking voice was saying, "It's a fine day to-day!" "A terribly fine day, Gilleasbuig," he said absently, then to the woman, "Do you know, Peigi Dhonn, what I am thinking? It has just come back to my mind that you were the very

first lass I married, after I came to Gleann Luachrach. And
—yes, I will say it—I don't believe you're a day less pretty
in all those years."

The minister was a very serious, even a very solemn man.
He would never laugh or be jocular and not often permitted
himself even a smile, although of recent years and on his
best days he would sometimes make a small and as it were
scriptural jest, as when he called a man's youngest son
" Benjamin." But for Maighstir Sachairi to be gallant, to pay
a compliment to a woman, was a thing unheard-of since he
came to Gleann Luachrach. Peigi Dhonn raised her eyes, and
there was a moment of amazement before she blushed and
looked pleased. The men for the first moment were amazed
also, then the constrained look passed like a cloud from their
faces. The miller was another who seldom smiled, but he was
smiling now. If Maighstir Sachairi did such a thing it could
be no ordinary day with him. And if so then for them also
it must be happy. They took it as a sign that he was not
troubled for the future, perhaps even that the danger had
passed already; and at once their hearts were lightened. The
miller let his glance rest affectionately on his wife who was
blushing and looking all at once surprisingly like a young
girl, and said, " That was only the first of many blessings I
have you to thank for, Maighstir Sachairi—although I won't
say that it wasn't one of the greatest." Gilleasbuigh Liath
laughed quietly in his beard, looking well pleased. When the
minister was gay it was as if God Himself had smiled, it was
a day for all men to be merry. And Maighstir Sachairi did
really appear to be in a gay humour; he seemed to become
light-hearted all at once when he paid the compliment to Peigi
Dhonn. He was looking now at the young children, the three
girls and the small, curly-haired boy, and beaming on them
as if he might suddenly have noticed that children were very
lovable. For their part the children unaware of his glance
were absorbed in finishing the porridge, the last morsels
were disappearing in quick succession into their mouths and
they were polishing the bowls with their spoons.

The miller said, " Here now are some trout, Maighstir Sachairi. The lad there caught them "—indicating the lad who had taken his horse and had now come in and sat down at the table.

The minister looked at his plate. " On my word! " he exclaimed, " these are the fine big fellows! " He turned to the lad. " Where did you catch them, Eachann? "

" At Poll a' Bhodaich, Maighstir Sachairi."

Maighstir Sachairi raised his eyebrows. " Indeed, you are telling me that? I wouldn't have thought you would get them so big up there."

" Oh, there are bigger ones at the Loop, just below Rosan Maol. But the Poll a' Bhodaich ones are sweeter, I think."

Maighstir Sachairi tasted a morsel in his mouth, savouring it thoughtfully. He gave an appreciative smack of the lips. " They *are* sweet! "

The lad, an overgrown freckled lad of about sixteen, the miller's second son—his first was in the army abroad—was flushing at once with embarrassment and pride that the minister was noticing him, consulting him, even seeming to defer to his judgment, and his parents and his grandfather were seeing it. Above all he was bursting with happiness because the minister condescended to enjoy and praise his fish.

" Oh, they are good enough, Maighstir Sachairi," he said in a deprecating voice. " Still it is hardly the month of May. In a few weeks they will be at their best and they will be really sweet."

Maighstir Sachairi smiled at his serious, grown-up air and looked across the table at the miller. " He is quite a fisher, the lad," he said, with an inclination of the head in the lad's direction.

" Oh, it's a great fisher that's in Eachann," said the miller, not without some paternal pride.

" Eachann would be fishing all the day," said Gilleasbuig Liath. " Oh, well," he added, " there's no harm in it for the lad. The fishing is very good employment for him. The disciples themselves were fishers in their day."

"That is true, Gilleasbuig," agreed Maighstir Sachairi. "One might say of the fishing that it is almost an apostolic employment." He turned again to the lad. "Well, Eachann, when it comes to the time that the Poll a' Bhodaich trout are at their best you must bring me some of them of your own catching till I see how good they are."

Eachann leant forward in his eagerness, his eyes shining with pleasure. He was aware of his mother smiling at him, proud of him; his father too and his grandfather. "I will do that, Maighstir Sachairi—and—thank you very much, Maighstir Sachairi," he managed to say, almost choking with happiness. The minister gave him a friendly look. He returned to his plate, saying in the same hearty, genial tone, "Well, I can now look forward with certainty to one other good breakfast in the days that are coming. How good God is to us poor sinners! He thinks even of the needs of our bellies, how He can satisfy our hunger with good things. For if we had only what we deserve it would not amount even to one breakfast."

"True. Oh true indeed!" Old Gilleasbuig sighed profoundly.

But the minister did not appear to have heard or to be disposed to continue his reflections; he had transferred his attention to the food before him and was eating with marvellous appetite. He began to praise the food, embarrassing Peigi Dhonn. Then he opened a conversation with the miller and Gilleasbuig Liath on the likelihood of good weather, and the state of the soil, the need now for a little rain; in so natural a manner that all were at once talking freely and at their ease. All except Peigi Dhonn who sat with her head lowered and said nothing, but lifted her eyes now and then to cast a shy but watchful glance under her dark brows at the minister. The young children although they gave no heed to what was being discussed could not be unaware of the whole atmosphere changed and lightened; they had become unconstrained, dared to lift their faces from their plates, even at last to carry on amongst themselves under the talk of their elders a conversation in nods and whispers.

On no previous occasion had Maighstir Sachairi condescended to be so genial. His brown eyes under their bushy brows without a trace of their wonted solemnity looked with a bright, interested expression into the face of the person who was speaking. He sat back at his ease, unashamedly taking snuff. He exchanged snuffboxes with Gilleasbuig Liath. More than once his glance went travelling about the room, as if from the low, blackened rafters to the door sneck and the chain dangling in the chimney he found everything very interesting.

When he got up to go the lad Eachann darted out of the house to get his horse and hold it for him. Gilleasbuig Liath took off his bonnet and held it on his knees, saying in reply to his salutation, " God's blessing with yourself, Maighstir Sachairi, till you come again! " The miller and Peigi Dhonn accompanied him to the door. When he had mounted and the lad let go the bridle he said, " Thank you, Eachann," and smiled down at him. He looked up at the miller and his wife standing in the doorway, the small children peering between them, and called out, " A thousand thanks to you! " The miller called back, " You are welcome, Maighstir Sachairi! We hope you will come again before it will be long! " Maighstir Sachairi smiled and raised his hand to his bonnet.

They stood watching the minister's sturdy form receding, the familiar strong back bobbing to the trot of the horse, until the gable edge cut off the view. Then the miller and his wife went inside. The miller was smiling. " Wasn't the minister the pleasant, hearty man to-day! " he said following his wife into the room.

The old man Gilleasbuig Liath had not moved, he was sitting looking reflectively straight before him, his hands still holding the bonnet on his knees. Perhaps some feeling of assurance had seemed to depart with Maighstir Sachairi. He said, " I hope nothing that will happen will cause the worthy man to come among us with a different face."

The miller was struck by that note of uncertainty. His

smile disappeared. "What then would happen to make Maighstir Sachairi change his face among us?"

The old man looked round. "Oh, nothing, Tormod. I don't know. I hope indeed that nothing will happen."

The miller looked at him a little longer, then his smile reappeared. "Och, now you will be frightening yourself. One had only to look at Maighstir Sachairi to-day to see that all that is over. Anybody could see it. Something has happened surely. It's my opinion the Black Foreigner is sitting at home just now biting his beard because Maighstir Sachairi has got the better of him, and it will be long before he shows his face in Gleann Luachrach."

The woman had gone and sat down on a low stool beside the hearth. She said softly, "God grant you may be right, Tormod."

The miller looked perplexed. "Do you doubt it, Peigi?"

She did not answer. After a moment she said inconsequently enough, "How changed he is now! Did you notice it, Tormod?"

The miller considered that. "He was different to-day certainly. He was free and hearty, he was pleased to be merry among us. Nobody ever saw him so free and hearty. Is that what you mean, Peigi?"

"No, that is not what I was meaning. Although he was different in that way too."

She looked up.

"His hair, Tormod! On his brow and temples, and here along his cheeks—it is quite grey! It was always red before, and now suddenly it is grey. Why do you think it would get grey so quickly?"

For an instant the miller was taken aback. Then he gave a little laugh. "Ach, Peigi! you were always a lass to be easily frightened. If the minister's hair is getting grey it will be because he is getting older. How old will he be now? He must be fifty, I would think. There is nothing in that. I have seen men getting grey when they had hardly passed the two score."

But he did not seem to have reassured Peigi Dhonn. She

looked away, saying in a thoughtful tone, "He is old all at once. His hair is grey now and his eyes are sunken in his head, his face is furrowed too. He looked like an old man to-day, although he was merry, hearty."

The miller waved his hand, turning to go out. "You are frightening yourself without cause or reason, lass. Maighstir Sachairi is only getting older. You can hardly blame him for that. But everything will be all right now. Wait a little and you will see." He went out to go to his work.

For a short time he stood in the sunshine looking at the fall in the river. The season was unusually dry and there was little water going over the fall, so that he next raised his head and looked about in the blue sky as if to see if there was promise of rain. Then he stepped across and looked down into the half-empty lade that brought the water to the wheel. He went into the mill and began to climb the ladder to the loft, feeling with his hands at the top because after the sunlight it was at first quite dark in here. In the loft it was a little lighter. Low down under the slates points of the sun entered and made lines across the dusty floor. The miller stood in the silence and the semi-dusk. He stood a long while quite still; a pencil of sunlight came slowly and picked out the edge of one trouser-leg from the calf downwards to the boot. He was seeing in his mind Maighstir Sachairi outfacing the Black Foreigner. Maighstir Sachairi was bending over him, his thin-lipped mouth compressed with indignation, shaking a finger and daring him to proceed so far as to harm a hair of one of his people. The Factor sitting bent forward in a chair, biting his lips with vexation, his angry face averted and scowling aside at the floor.

He stood enjoying the pleasant picture; then straightening himself stepped over and began to draw some heavy bags of grain out of a corner. A little later the three youngest of his children in the course of their play scampered in at the door of the mill and stopped suddenly, looking at each other in alarm. Their father was moving about at his work in the loft above them—and he was whistling at the top of his breath, "*Ho-ro mo Bhobug an Dram!*" The great man their father, stern, severe, the greatest after Maighstir Sachairi and God—and he was whistling!

* * * *

Maighstir Sachairi did not ride far after leaving the house of the mill. He was looking about, seeming to be enjoying the perfection of the spring day that filled the sunny valley, and his eye fell on a large clump of trees or small wood standing by the river bank. Because the young leaves were new-opened and tender, and the sun was shining among and through them, the tops and branches seemed to shed about a pale green light. It beckoned him, this sunny spot, and without hesitation or reflection he obeyed an impulse to visit it, and turned his horse. Dismounting on the outskirts he threw the rein over the crook of a low branch and went forward among the trees. Here he walked under a roof of translucent greenness with small blue openings on the sky, and the ground and the tree-trunks were gold spangled. The rustling of the leaves fell over him with a faint sound like coolness of spray. At the small wood's farther edge the river came hurrying round a bend into a still, deep pool. There he sat down on a flat rock at the edge of the trees and began to look meditatively into the pool, where at the shallow side the sun made visible brown weed-covered stones shelving steeply into the depths. The sun making his presence felt.

But he had scarcely settled in its warmth to a pleasant, full-fed languor when a grisly shape of recollection invaded his contentment. It had *not* been disposed of, that thing. It lurked. And here it came. An unpleasant awareness of himself came creeping over him. He got hurriedly to his feet and threw a startled glance behind, over this shoulder and that. And now the sunlight seemed unkind, and the river and the leafy trees were no longer an eyes'-delight; rather he had the impression that in that glance something repulsive had momentarily shown itself behind their seeming innocence. As if he had detected Evil lurking under the display of pleasant Spring. And with his breast full of alarm he hurried from the spot.

He emerged from the little wood at the side opposite to the place where he had left his horse and walked rapidly up the glen. . . . He could not understand now that state from which he had awakened; nor how he had come to conduct himself as he had for the last few hours. Once he looked up, and frowned and curled his lip at the pleasant scene that he saw. Thenceforward he kept his eyes on the ground, and quickened his pace. He recalled his conduct in the miller's house, how he had jested and taken his ease, and he marvelled at himself. His words and actions came back to mind, and they shocked him. He saw himself laughing, grinning, nodding his head up and down, waving his arms about with large, unrestrained gestures, surprising everybody and putting them out of countenance by persisting in his undignified behaviour. He remembered Peigi Dhonn's face and how she had looked at him and blushed with shame and embarrassment. The shame, he felt sure, had been for him; nor could he wonder. A minister of the gospel behaving like a worldling, using the language of a seducer and a reprobate—it was a shameful spectacle. Looking back upon it he could feel himself accompanying those light and wanton words with a look, sly and knowing. He quickened his pace still more as if he would have walked away from the recollection. He was astounded now to think of such forgetfulness as had overtaken him. His recent cheerfulness appeared incomprehensible.

He stopped, stood looking at the ground. In a lucid pause he had perceived when this came. From that one Uncertainty. It had destroyed every sureness, dividing his mind. Since then he had been of two judgments in everything. If he could not divide the Hand of God from the work of Satan, how could he tell what was right in *any* instance? whether to be stern, or social; to eat, or to refrain from eating; to go into this room, or not to go; to stand up, or remain seated. He could not put his hand to his mouth without a moral struggle and a smart of conscience. From that one Uncertainty his judgment was all unseated, and his mind reeled before the possibilities involved in the simplest and most natural act;

for spirit is not Size and in the smallest act could be a whole universe of sin.

In a moment he had set off again, walking rapidly. Now it was the need for haste that burdened him. He could not forgive himself for having wasted a single precious moment in levity. A powerful impression forced itself upon his mind that all the time he was jesting and talking foolishly in the miller's house there had been something, something of importance, that he ought to have been doing. What it was did not appear, he could not stop to consider it, but hurried on, feeling that he must make haste now if he was not to be too late. And now he could not fail any longer to be aware of how his heart was beating furiously. The fact surprised him, because his body was strong and active and exertion had never formerly tried him. Now he was breathless. . . .

Coming to the little slope where the smithy stood he turned aside and began to ascend. He did this knowing in his mind that he had seen the smith among the men driving cattle to the Machair, yet he continued to labour upward, his breath coming painfully. He went into the hut knowing in himself that the smith could not be there—and when he saw that it was so, collapsed on to a bench feeling that here was a check, and how was he to get over it! Afterwards he remembered that moment in particular for the wave of despondency that overcame him, such despondency as he had never known. He felt that here at last he was at the end of himself, his hope, his help, his strength and resources; the dark night swung down upon his soul. It flooded in upon him darkly, drowning him under a wave of fear and helplessness. He was sitting on the bench in the smithy and with his right hand he was clutching his breast. Choking now. Afraid of a nothingness that wanted him. He was aware that his eyes were starting and staring. And all help divine or human was not where he was. To his growing accustomed eyes forms of objects began to come out of the dusk with a looming presence—tools, a heavy hammer leaning leaningly against the anvil, the bellows-handle jutting in a transverse gesture over him—each sizing forward with a secret-hostile *adsum*ness.

And present, breathing about, beard-scorched and blackened in the smoke, broad metal-smelled—the *sigh* of the smith.

It passed. It was only a moment. Strangely then, his one desire was for sleep. A heavy lethargy settled down over him, but pleasant, and the coming sleep would be profound, releasing. He desired it with a great longing, towards forgetfulness. His eyelids dropped . . . closed. . . . At once he was stark awake again. And there it was! It took him as always in the middle of the breast and mounted quickly into the throat—an excitement and constriction, with perturbation and the sense of something left undone. He gazed about, and saw that he was sitting in inactivity when it was a time to *do* —and little time, little time, now. This urgency was like something outside himself which forced him to his feet and out into the air. And away, walking rapidly. . . .

Once he stopped on a little bridge over a tributary streamlet and stood looking attentively at the glen, up and own. There were few people to be seen. Here and there were groups of children among the fields, posted there to prevent the remaining cattle from invading them and eating the brear of springing corn. Now and then some wife in a white currachd appeared and disappeared about the doors of the crofts and outbuildings standing on the slopes. Otherwise he was quite alone in this upper region of the glen. The burn below him made its own glug-ing and gurgling noise running to join the river. Occasionally the voices of the nearer children came to his ear as they shouted in their games. For the rest the glen lay in sunbathed silence. Maighstir Sachairi was looking at everything very attentively, saying over to himself the names of the crofts on the hillsides and the farms to be seen farther down where the glen was wider: Druim Dearg, Tom a' Mhadaidh, Baile Sheumais, Aird Mhór, Bail' nan Tobar, Ach' a' Choirce, Baile Mhic Eoin. . . .

He raised his hand and stood a moment pressing the palm against his brow. Then with a peculiar gesture drew the hand, slowly, down his face.

He turned and resumed his rapid walking.

The glen got narrower. The crofts were left behind. Last of all there was a ridge jutting forward almost into the centre of the valley and ending in an abrupt rocky face over-hanging the river; and perched on the summit a low thatched dwelling. Without a moment's hesitation he turned aside along the path. He crossed the plank bridge over the river, which was here an inconsiderable but noisy stream, and mounted the steep short path to the crown of the ridge. When he reached the top he was again breathless and gasp-ing and his heart pounding in his breast. But he hurried on.

He had reached the hither side of a low barn or outhouse when he suddenly drew up. He had been walking all the way with his eyes on the ground, he now raised his head and began glancing about as if he were surprised at where he found himself—as if he had wakened from sleep in this strange place. When he had looked a while he made a move-ment of turning back, then seemed to change his mind. He walked towards the dwelling.

But had only passed the farther wall of the low outhouse when something caused him to glance aside—and he leapt back a pace and stood wide-eyed, staring.

For his part the white-haired and white-bearded old man seemed to have been a trifle startled too. He stood staring back at the minister, his body bent slightly forward, the axe held with both hands above his head as it had been arrested in act to strike.

The old man was first to recover. With an energy almost shocking in one of his years he brought down the axe so that the head sank deep in the block on which he had been chopping wood. He grunted as he struck the blow.

Then he came forward.

" Ah! You have come then, Maighstir Sachairi! "

CHAPTER SEVEN

MAIGHSTIR SACHAIRI could hardly restrain his irritation. The moment he came in and sat down he had begun to be conscious of it, a strange uneasiness and irritability which made him want to cry out upon the old man at every word or leap up and fly from the room. Yet he was too irritated to be capable of getting up and going from the room. To his greater and greater annoyance he still sat still and went on replying and continuing the conversation, trying to restrain himself.

At a little distance there might have seemed nothing particularly noticeable about the other man; an ordinary-looking old man, small of stature, and with a slight halt or hirple in his gait. But he was no sooner seen close at hand than he began to make a very singular impression. That impression was not the result of any striking feature or physical peculiarity, which might remain unnoticed at a distance but became visible on a near approach. It came from no feature in particular, but was felt as a general impression, as it were from the man *himself*. He was one of those whose presence cannot be overlooked. If he entered a company, even by stealth and unobserved, everyone would shortly become aware as if by some message of a mysterious sense, that *somebody* had come among them. In such a case particular characteristics matter little. The man was exceedingly neat and well-proportioned, for his obvious age surprisingly erect and active. His features were refined and pleasing. But in Gleann Luachrach strong, active bodies and well-cut features were the rule. What made this man outstanding was felt rather as an energy or intensity of his being, a certain vividness of the self, an essential vigour, which informed

both movement and repose and was striking in every glance
of the strangely light, blue eyes.

Maighstir Sachairi's rising irritation had reached the point
where his very hands shook, he felt he must lose control of
himself. He had thought it was the man's voice, his persis-
tence in maintaining conversation, that was irritating him so
strangely, in spite of himself and his effort to remain calm;
at every politely spoken sentence he had the impulse to fly
out of his chair and shout at him, contradict him, silence
him. But his silence now affected him with a four-fold irritation. He was on the point of letting himself go completely,
and he did not know what would happen. He directed at
the old man a glance of such concentrated anger that he
felt his eyeballs burn with it, and his whole body tremble.
Maighstir Sachairi had felt himself shouting; now that he
was not speaking he felt he had shouted very loudly indeed,
he could hear his voice, almost screaming. Anybody must
have noticed it. He looked at the old man, and his lips
curled with angry contempt. What an attempt at deception!
he thought: he sits there with his hands clasped round his
knee letting on to meditate, and thinks to make me believe
he never noticed I raised my voice above a whisper!

With that another thought entered his mind. This Fearchar
is a sly fellow, he thought to himself, he is up to something
now, I must be prepared for him. . . . He began to watch
him suspiciously, stealthily.

The old man sat on a low stool opposite, his side-face
to the minister, seeming quite unconscious of the glances
directed on him. One foot was stretched out towards the little
fire on the hearth; with his hands clasped round the other
knee he was swaying his body gently backwards and forwards. The attitude was striking, it was very youthful. In
him it expressed the greatest naturalness and freedom, an
inner freedom, of the personality, perfectly inoffensive in the
presence of one to be respected. Looking serenely at the fire
he seemed one whom the next thing that happened could
never irritate or perturb, for he would be instantly ready to

accept it. He might have been humming to himself there, swaying very gently to and fro.

"I think you are inclined to be suspicious of me still, Maighstir Sachairi!"

Maighstir Sachairi was startled. The man is a very fiend, he thought, he even knows my thoughts. He said nothing, looking watchfully.

"Maybe you think I bear ill-will to you: it would be very natural if you thought that, even after all the years that have passed since then. But no; I never bore you a grudge. It is true that for a long time I was going about feeling like a lost man—that was afterwards, when every man was with you and against me—and at first I was inclined to resent that a little. But you can understand how I would feel like that. You see, you had made me an exile and a friendless man in the place where formerly—I don't say it from pride—I had been a leader. But somehow I could never blame you in my heart, and afterwards I came to accept it that things had happened so, and that *as* they had happened *so* they must be."

Maighstir Sachairi thought: Let me only discover what game he is playing; if I wait he is bound to give himself away. . . .

The old man resumed. "I can guess what you are thinking, Maighstir Sachairi. Yes, I understood all the time that it was pride that kept me away, I understood it quite well. But I thought at the first that it was *due* to my pride not to hasten to put myself in your road after I had been opposing you with the people and you had won the day. That was what I thought: but I am not excusing myself. And now since I would not come to you, you have been so magnanimous as to come to me—after those many years. I see that you are above me also in generosity, Maigshtir Sachairi. I see now that it would have been better if I had been more humble."

With every word Maighstir Sachairi's suspicions became confirmed: he thought, Humility does not become you, Poet! He felt certain now that he was being played with, that the old man knew something, or had some motive behind his mildness. With that certainty came another feeling, a feeling that he was to be trapped! He began to wish to escape, he felt he must get up and go—now—before it was too late.

His voice said, rather surlily, "You must ask forgiveness from God. It is against His will you offended."

The old man neither moved nor looked up, but continued to gaze meditatively into the little fire. All at once Maighstir Sachairi was startled by a sound. He was certain that, in the silence, he had heard a sound, a long-drawn, tragic sound, like a sigh. He glanced quickly round expecting to see someone in the room. There was no one. His glance returned to the other. Could it have come from him?

The old man was speaking again, in a meek voice. "I would like to ask you a question, Maighstir Sachairi. . . . Can the will of God be known for certain in particular circumstances?"

Maighstir Sachairi looked at him. He is trying to catch me, he thought. I won't speak another word to him; if he speaks to me I will not answer.

He said, "Certainly it can be known."

"What is the guide, Maighstir Sachairi?"

"The Word."

"Does the Word, then, give certain guidance in every circumstance that may arise in the lives of men?"

"In every circumstance. The Bible is the only guide God has given or will give, and it contains all the guidance necessary for all men in all times." Maighstir Sachairi felt certain that with every word he spoke he was involving himself more hopelessly. He wanted to ignore the questions, to get up and go from the room without a word or look more for this old man who began to appear terrible to him, with his mild voice and inoffensive air and his heart within him black with guile. Instead he sat still answering every question with alacrity, he even found himself taking pains to make his answers clear and easy to be understood.

The old man had been seeming to ponder his last reply.

He said, " But there might be different interpretations of
the Word? "

" But only one true one," said Maighstir Sachairi.

" Then there must needs be some sure way of knowing
that true interpretation. How is it to be known, Maighstir
Sachairi? "

" By the Holy Spirit."

The old man pondered that. " You will be thinking me a
very ignorant man, Maighstir Sachairi," he said. While he
said it Maighstir Sachairi felt sure he detected a faint smile
that instantly disappeared. " I will take the liberty of asking a
question more: Do all have the Spirit? "

" It is given to the Elect."

" Do the Elect receive the Spirit at birth? " he asked. " Or
must they obtain it? "

" They receive it after they are converted, when they
accept Christ." All the time he listened for and answered the
questions Maighstir Sachairi was saying in his own mind:
What is he leading up to? I should know this! He is going
to trap me. When I met him there he said " You have
come then! "—in such a tone. He must have expected me
therefore: he has laid his plans, and is going to trap me. . . .

The old man was saying, " Do the Elect always have the
Spirit thereafter? "

" They may lose the help and guidance for a time if they
walk unworthily and grieve the Spirit," said Maighstir
Sachairi. If I do not go I am lost, he thought.

" Have patience with me a little longer, Maighstir Sachairi;
let me see if I have understood it all. . . . The only way in
which the will of God can be known is from the Bible, which
is the Word of God and contains somewhere or other within
it a certain and infallible guidance for every circumstance
that may arise in the lives of men. But what that guidance
is can only be discerned in the Word by the aid of the Spirit,
which is an inner light of interpretation possessed only by the
Elect."

" It is even so."

Maighstir Sachairi no longer hoped to be able to get up and go. He sat in his chair as if held there. He even found himself listening with a kind of eagerness for the question that would come next.

He heard the old man speaking—" But that Spirit and inward light may be withdrawn, you say? "

" It may."

The old man pondered that. He began again to sway his body gently backwards and forwards. When he spoke again Maighstir Sachairi was sure he used a different tone, and that there was some significance in that.

" The important question then seems to be whether the Spirit can be withdrawn from one of the Elect *without his knowing*."

Maighstir Sachairi did not reply at once. He was pondering the question, but chiefly he was trying to get behind it. Almost before the other spoke he had said to himself, This is it now! He felt certain the trap was laid for him in that question and was casting feverishly about in his mind to discover it. What exasperated him most of all was that he felt he knew it all the time, yet could not grasp it before it was necessary to reply. It never occurred to him not to answer, that he need not answer.

But he was silent so long that it must have seemed to the other that he would not answer, for all at once he was aware of him speaking. He gave a start of something like apprehension when he heard the voice. Then after a few sentences it dawned on him that the old man had changed the subject and was talking of other matters. He experienced a great relief when he understood this. He breathed, and only then realised that all the time he was considering that last question he had been holding his breath. But he had been too certain he was almost caught there to be all at once reassured; he would have to be wary, he thought.

" Do you know, Maighstir Sachairi," the old man was saying, " it is really surprising the thoughts and reflections that a man will have who is much with himself. At first, maybe—when he first begins to be often alone—it is only the things that belong to his own life that he will be thinking about: his beasts, the spring work, when he will mend the thatch, when he will go fishing. . . . But the man is long alone. When he has thought about all that, there is not enough in it to occupy a mind. . . . Yet he must always be thinking. . . . And so in the end such a man will fall to reflecting for long periods, in his solitude, upon great and high matters—upon universal things, Maighstir Sachairi; the world, and man's life, and why things are as they are, and the purposes that will be moving behind the changes that he sees. Long thoughts he will have, a man like that, about former times, and the fortunes of men and nations. . . . In the end the universal things, the things that all men share, will begin to seem more important to that lonely man than his own concerns. It will even seem—this is a strange thing, Maighstir Sachairi—it will even seem to him as if the mind were doing what is most natural to it when it is occupied with those high things, and not when it is considering the things that belong only to his own life. . . . It will go so far with him that those great matters he considers in his mind will begin to seem more *real* than the things he sees and touches. . . . "

" I suppose that might be so," said Maighstir Sachairi guardedly, with a wary look from the sides of his eyes.

" Yes, Maighstir Sachairi, as time went on and one year followed another I was more and more pondering those high things. I would be sitting here for hours after other, even forgetting to eat. Or sitting on the hillside." He smiled as if at a recollection. " Once I stood for a whole day in the barn—that bothan where I met you just now. I went in for some corn I was to grind in the brà—it was in the morning, the sun was rising—and it was dark when I came to myself, I had to feel my way out to the door. . . . But no matter about that," he said, becoming serious again. " I don't mean that I am able to answer those questions that I am always pondering, I don't mean that at all. Naturally I am often unable to reach any answer that satisfies me; I am an unlearned man. That is why I am taking the oppor-

tunity of your being here to ask those questions, Maighstir
Sachairi. It is simply that I want to know."

Maighstir Sachairi eyed him.

" For instance, Maighstir Sachairi—if you will not be
angry with me for mentioning a thing that has been a cause
of disagreement between us. . . . The songs, and the music—
the pleasure that can be taken in them. . . . "

" Vanity! " Maighstir Sachairi interrupted, abruptly and
angrily. " Sin and vanity! Such are not to be talked about! "

" Even so, Maighstir Sachairi; sin and vanity! " the old
man agreed, unperturbed. " Therein lies the difficulty I am
speaking of. . . . It is not that such things—poetry and
music—give pleasure;—for we know there are many things
that give a kind of pleasure and yet are most clearly sins,
for they degrade the one that enjoys them, or they harm
another. The difficulty is, that a man experiences the pleasure
of poetry and music *as if it were something good for him*—
and *yet* it is vanity and a sin! Have patience with me,
Maighstir Sachairi. I know very clearly in my mind what I
want to say, but these are difficult matters and I have not
your skill of words. Maybe I can show you what I mean. . . .
Consider, for instance, a man that is drunken. He knows
beforehand that it is both a sin and against reason. Yet he
drinks more than is right, and gets pleasure in it. But he
makes himself a worse man than he was before, he knows
that, and while doing harm to himself he makes others suffer
too. So it is easy to see that drunkenness and the pleasure
of drunkenness is a sin. The man knows it himself, for he
experiences the results of it as an evil. But it is otherwise
with poetry or making music. In this case a man feels an
urge of his mind and as it were his very being to make a
poem or song out of an experience that he has, an experience
of the beauty of the world, maybe, or of love to a woman or
his country: or in hearing music or a poem a man sees and
experiences as the man did who made it. There is pleasure in
that too, great pleasure. But it is unlike the pleasure of being
drunken, for it is lasting and not a deception. And it makes
a man that experiences it better, not worse, than he was

before. Or so it seems to him. He feels stirred, lifted up in his mind and spirit—as if his *soul* were made bigger. He goes from it with love in his heart to all men, so that he will do a favour to the first man he meets, or if it is his enemy he will forgive him gladly. It seems he is both a better man in himself and others benefit from it. There for you is my difficulty, Maighstir Sachairi. . . . Poetry and music are sinful, we say—yet with poetry and music a man improves himself in his nature it seems. How is that? How is it that a thing that is undoubtedly sinful should both appear as something to be desired, and still seem a good when possessed? How is it that a sin can be experienced as *a good*, as something that makes larger and purifies the soul? so that— in these cases—you might say a man seems to become all ways better by dint of sinning."

Maighstir Sachairi had been showing signs of a growing restlessness while the old man was speaking, pausing now and then to consider his words. He answered rather testily, in a tone of impatience. " There is no difficulty at all about your question; since it is troubling you I will answer it. You are only forgetting the principal thing, and that is, the Fall. Firstly:—Why do you find in your music and poetry and vanity a pleasure which is not like the pleasure of drunkenness and other vices but is lasting and appears to you a good and to be desired? The answer is: Because the nature of man's mind finds satisfaction in these vanities— his *whole* nature, his nature *itself*, not only his senses for a little as in drunkenness. It is simply that man's nature is inclined to such vanities as poetry and music to the end of its satisfaction, to be satisfied in them. And because a man's nature finds its satisfaction in them, so they appear to him a good and to be desired. And secondly:—Why are they yet sinful? The answer is, For the same reason—that they are a satisfaction of man's nature. For by the Fall man's Nature—that nature to which such vanities are a good, and which you say grows larger by them—that nature is itself in sin and utterly depraved. Because by Adam's fall man is in sin by his very nature, and all expression of that nature and everything that ministers to its satisfaction are therefore Sin, and an offence to God, to be punished with damnation unless God freely choose to save that man." At the last words Maighstir Sachairi smote his hand twice on the arm of the chair. By this time his suspicion and fear had been forgotten and his angry irritation had returned.

The old man did not appear to notice the noise Maighstir Sachairi made with his hand· or the way his voice was rising in a note of irritation. Not looking at him but still keeping his eyes on the fire he listened with an air of respectful attention. He nodded his head gravely. "That is well answered, Maighstir Sachairi."

After seeming for a while to fall again into thought, he said, "Although it never occurred to me as the answer to that question, I have thought much too about the Fall. There is another question there that troubles me. I would like to ask you . . . if it wouldn't be too much. . . ."

He seemed to await permission. Maighstir Sachairi said nothing, but looked at him irritably, knitting his brows.

"Then since you permit it, Maighstir Sachairi. . . . It is about the nature of man which is, as you truly say, utterly depraved, so that every expression of it is sinful and an offence to God. It is easy to understand that so long as it has to do with sinful men, such as—God help me—I am myself. But it is different . . . there is, to my mind, a difficulty . . . when it is thought of in connection with good men, men that were saints. Consider one of them, for instance; one who, as you might say, pleased God. The Apostle Paul, for instance. We know how he was a wicked man and persecuted the saints. Then the Lord met him, that time, on the road to Damascus, and he was converted; and afterwards he was a great apostle, going everywhere teaching and preaching the Gospel. Now here is my difficulty, Maighstir Sachairi—I seem to see in Saul that persecuted and Paul the Apostle the same man, *and with the same nature*. He was a strong man, eloquent, very fearless. That was his nature, and it is easy to understand that it was depraved and sinful, when he was using it for persecuting the saints of God. But when he was converted it does not seem that his nature was in any way changed, for as a saint he appears the same man, and even more eloquent and more fearless. How then; Maighstir Sachairi—the Apostle's eloquence and the acts of his strength and fearlessness were expressions of his nature, which by the Fall was utterly depraved; would it be right to say then that they were sinful and displeasing to God, even when they were being greatly used in His service? "

Maighstir Sachairi's irritation was at last breaking out of control. He almost shouted, " Great is your ignorance, old man! It is not flattering to me to find the like in my parish. Paul the Apostle was just as much a sinful man on the day he died as was Saul of Tarsus when he kept the clothes of them that stoned Stephen. He was not saved by his eloquence or acts of courage, but his sins were covered by the Blood of Christ. He was saved by Grace, and Grace is contrary to Nature—every little child in Gleann Luachrach knows so much."

It was becoming impossible to appear not to notice Maighstir Sachairi's angry tone. The old man Fearchar bowed his head a little. He said even more mildly, " You teach me humility, Maighstir Sachairi. What am I to do when even the children in Gleann Luachrach know more of sacred things than I do myself who am an old man! I can only ask you to have patience with me, for if you do not answer the questions that are in my mind there is no on else that will.

" There is another question yet, Maighstir Sachairi. . . . I am afraid you will think it a foolish question too. . . . If man's nature *itself* is sinful, then it seems clear there can be no degrees of good or bad in human conduct, but *all* acts of a man are equally sin in the eyes of God, since they all proceed from that nature. If so, and if we are saved or damned in spite of anything we have done, then I cannot—forgive me, Maighstir Sachairi—I am so foolish that I cannot see what reason is left for demanding from men certain kinds of conduct as against others. But since it can make no difference to our eternal welfare, since no good act can come from a nature evil at its root—and we are saved anyway, or damned—would that not be a reason why men should live while they are in this world the kind of life that seems all ways best, in peace and friendliness with their neighbours, Elect and Damned together, and in the enjoyment of those things that are harmless and enrich their natures, judging things and events whether they be just or unjust and so opposing the evil man and the oppressor till peace and justice rule in the land? "

" That's you now, Poet! " Maighstir Sachairi was leaning forward out of his chair, his face red. " You were known of old for your arguing and reasoning! If the Wicked One wanted one man in Alba that could make his ways appear reasonable and like wholesome truth the man would be yourself, and he would not be disappointed in you. But you get no nearer the Truth with your subtlety. God is not accountable to us, to make His ways conformable to sinful human reason; God's ways and God's justice are contrary to human reason and man's justice. And as He freely chooses to save some and damn others and not according to their works, so He demands certain kinds of conduct of all men whether Elect or reprobate according to His pleasure and not according to what seems reasonable to man, and so also He orders things not according to human justice. He has the right. Your reason is nothing."

" God's reason is contrary to man's reason and God's justice is contrary to man's justice! " The poet repeated it to himself in a kind of thoughtful amazement. " If that is so there is nothing that can be said. . . . "

" It *is* so! ! "

The old man gave a little start and a flicker of his eyes in the minister's direction, but otherwise betrayed no sign that a voice had suddenly shouted angrily almost in his ear.

On the contrary he at once made a slight movement of turning towards the minister, though still without looking at him, and said in a fresh voice briskly—quite as if the latter conversation had not taken place—" I have forgotten, Maighstir Sachairi. . . . Did you say that the light of the

Spirit could be withdrawn from one of the Elect *without his knowing it*?"

Maighstair Sachairi was caught at unawares and completely taken aback. His jaw dropped. He stammered, "If he had been careless . . . that could be so . . . if he had not been examining his life . . . yes . . . for a time . . . in certain circumstances."

"It *is* possible then, even for one of the Elect—Maighstir Sachairi—to be mistaken as to whether a thing is according to the will of God or not?"

No reply came from Maighstir Sachairi. His face had gone ashen, his eyes stared at his inquisitor in a kind of fascination. He was making some movements as if he were trying to rise out of his chair.

The old man abandoned his easy attitude. He rested a hand on each knee and leant forward. He might have appeared by his posture to be demanding an answer from the fire.

"You don't answer, Maighstir Sachairi. Maybe I am not making myself clear. Forgive me; how I regret that I am not a learned man! I will try to make it clearer. . . . Supposing, for instance, an event were about to take place, an event, let us say, that would be a great calamity to many innocent people, and to avert it it was necessary first of all and above everything to know whether it was the will of God or not; is it possible—I only ask in order to know—is it possible even for one of the Elect to make a mistake and suppose that event to be according to the will of God while in truth it is opposed and contrary to God's will?"

Although he did not look round he seemed to listen. . . .

When at last Maighstir Sachairi spoke his voice was hardly recognisable, and so low that it almost whispered.

"It . . . is . . . possible. . . ."

2

At that some extraordinary commotion and loud pandemonium broke loose. For it seemed to Maighstir Sachairi that the house was tumbling down about him. The air shook.

His ears rang, his nerves and senses reeled and jangled in its loud metallic clamour. And he had only time to think, before the intruding presence would engulf him suddenly; *He* is here! the Evil One, his Master! Fearchar the Poet had disappeared in a moment, gone out in the blinding yellow light that flashed before his eyes. He could not see him. But the thought in his mind was: He knows! He knows my very inmost thoughts! By his Master's power whom he serves he knows them! . . .

The noise was caused by the old man Fearchar. He had bent forward to make up the fire, and had let the tongs drop from his hand to the hearthstone.

Gradually Maighstir Sachairi came to himself in his chair, seeing the Poet in his place. He was deliberately building the red hearts of peats, separated from the surrounding ash; into a glowing cone. Then building the fresh turfs about them. His strongly nervous hand wielding the tongs, deliberately; the legs of it opening, feeling about, closing and carrying. Maighstir Sachairi watched all from a great distance, knowing what he would do next, inevitably. And not at once did he realise that what he now saw was truly the continuation of the same world and time in which he had sat before; that there was no strangeness stirring, but that he had only looked at things familiar and most ordinary for a moment unfamiliarly; that he sat here, and saw Fearchar, his enemy of twenty years, in the veritable, common act of building the fire; and that therefore his shock and perturbation were not from things but of his own disordered feeling.

Fearchar sat upright, dusting his hands together. Then he settled himself leaning forward with an elbow on each knee, his hands clasped between them. Some time he looked pensively at the fire, until he began to smile his soft, reminiscent smile. He began to speak; Maighstir Sachairi recognised the air and tone of a man who would make conversation and entertain a guest.

"One question I was pondering that time I stood for a whole day in the barn—it would be about the month of March. . . . Since then I have often pondered it. . . . Suppose

there are two nations, Maighstir Sachairi. Two nations that
are neighbours; and one of them bigger than the other and
more numerous. . . . The larger nation is trying to conquer
and bring into subjection the one that is smaller. But the
men of the little nation are very brave and devoted to freedom, and although they may often be defeated by greater
numbers on the field of battle they will always rise and fight
again. So the big nation can never subject them, because
they are determined never to be conquered. But now suppose that the big nation understands at last that it is no use
to try to conquer them by force of arms. Suppose they try
another way. For instance they may pretend to be friendly
and by some trick get power over the smaller nation and
unite them to themselves. And so they will get with pretended friendship and a trick what they could never win by
war and arms."

Maighstir Sachairi heard every word, quite clearly. He
understood without difficulty what each word meant. But of
what all in their order signified he had no notion, nor made
the least effort to understand. Long before (as it seemed),
shortly after his sitting down, and when the conversation went
as yet tardily as between two strangers or men upon their
guard, there had suddenly occurred to him what at once
appeared the strangest and most startling thing. It was
simply that he was *here*, in this man's house: and for the
second time that day he had had the sensation of coming
unpleasantly to himself after a period in which he had acted
unaccountably, as in a dream. That feeling and intimate and
unclothed recognition had now returned; he looked about,
and found his presence there extraordinarily strange. Strange,
and stranger still, familiar. For in spite of the marvellous
and unfamiliar aspect under which the occasion looked at
him, it had yet a quality about it of awakened recollection.
Sometime, he was suddenly feeling, all this happened before!
(At this moment, for the first time, it occurred to him that
he might be ill). He even felt he could anticipate the conversation of the Poet—did not need to listen to him, for he
knew beforehand the words that he would say. . . .

" This now is the question, Maighstir Sachairi. When the two nations—the bigger and the smaller—are united, so that the government of the larger one rules both, what would be the likely thing to happen then? Would that be the end of the struggle between them? Would the big nation be satisfied when it had taken away the freedom of the little nation and got control over it, and would they then at last leave its people in peace to live freely in their own land after their own fashion and the customs of their forefathers? Or would there be in truth no difference?—the big nation would go on and not rest till it had utterly destroyed and eaten up the little nation, harrying its people from the land and uprooting them until nothing was left, neither land nor people—except that now it would commit at its leisure, under pretext of government and with forms of Law, the devastations it made in former times with invading armies, and the little nation would not now be able to resist it? It is an interesting question, Maighstir Sachairi. What would be your opinion? "

When the answer came even Fearchar the Poet was startled out of his composure. He had scarcely begun to describe his question—speaking in an easy, friendly tone, like a man who would draw into conversation a loth and silent guest—when a change came over Maighstir Sachairi. Recovering from the shock and the moment when the house seemed to be dissolving about him with resounding clangour he had sat for a little in a kind of composure of exhaustion, leaning back limply in his chair regarding the Poet and his movements with a dull impersonality. With almost the same listless-seeming glance he turned his eyes finding the place and the occasion at once marvellously strange and strangely familiar. But even as the other began to describe his question his look altered. As if some entirely new thought had struck him he turned to looking at the Poet in an intent and searching manner, staring at his face, as if he would have got some answer out of him by his will, by staring hard at him. He was visibly labouring under some intense excitement, his hands clasping and unclasping themselves nervously on the knobs of the chair arms. He rose to an upright

position in the chair, then leaned forward as if he would
have interrupted; but although his lips moved no sound
came. The old man had finished speaking before he found a
voice. But it was not *his* voice. An unnatural, croaking thing
said . . . " Were you . . . I *demand* to know . . . Once and for
all—*Did you know that I would come*?" The old man
jerked round his head and saw the face near him, pale, the
eyes feverish, the lips compressed and twitching.

In an instant he was on his feet, at his small height. " But
Maighstir Sachairi . . . You are ill! " His blue eyes were
wide with alarm and concern. He made a motion of wringing
his hands. " I, the fool . . . Maighstir Sachairi . . .! " He
turned quickly and crossed the room with his small uneven
steps.

Maighstir Sachairi lay back heavily in his chair with every
appearance of exhaustion. He drew a hand wearily along
his brow, wet with a cold sweat. When the old man came
back he languidly waved the glass aside.

" But Maighstir Sachairi, you are ill. It will do you good!"
Maighstir Sachairi glanced up at him standing over him
solicitously, and shook his head.

" Put it down . . . Or take it yourself, rather. I am not
ill." He put his hand to his brow and sat, his hand covering
his eyes.

In a little he took his hand away and looked up, and
Fearchar was standing there still, regarding him with a
concerned gravity. Maighstir Sachairi drew his brows together. " Sit down now," he said weakly, in a kind of wearied
irritation. " You were talking about something. There is
nothing wrong with me." He put his hand to his brow again.

The old man looked down at him doubtfully. Then turning
he put down the glass with the whisky on the table edge,
where it would be within reach. He returned to the fire,
giving another slow glance at the minister. Then he lifted
the stool where it had overturned when he jumped up in his
alarm and sitting down on it in his former place settled
himself quietly like a man settling himself to wait.

" Why are you not speaking? " Maighstir Sachairi's voice

broke in in an ordinary tone, though weak still. "You were saying something . . . about nations . . . two nations. Go on then, I am listening. And speak plainly," he added with a weak return of irritation. " Don't speak in parables! "

The old man took a final glance at him. Then as if he decided that Maighstir Sachairi really wished him to go on he turned away; he clasped his hands round his knee in his accustomed posture and began swaying his body almost imperceptibly backwards and forwards.

He smiled. "I see it is no use trying to deceive you, Maighstir Sachairi. You are a man with whom it is best to be open from the beginning! " The apologetic smile became sad, and faded out.

"Yes, I really was speaking all the time about this . . . this thing, this that has happened in Gleann Mór and the Srath Meadhonach. That was what I had in my mind; you saw through that. And what the Black Factor swears he will do to us in Gleann Luachrach too. . . . "

Here a spasm of some powerful emotion seemed to pass across his features.

Recovering his calm he went on.

"I am looking back over the history of our nation, Maighstir Sachairi. . . . " By his tone and brooding air it seemed as if he saw it all before him.

" I look back, and what is it I see there, in that past! I see war and fighting, disaster upon disaster, the blood of the Albannaich poured out on the soil of every century, I see strifes, invasions, famines, burnings, sorrow on sorrow—who can count them!

" But how is this?—Am I mistaken, or do I truly see the great-part of those sorrows that they are bound together and are but one, one long sorrow? I do not speak of Romanaich and Lochlannaich, whom the forefathers hurled backwards. But what is the cause of war and battles, and bloodshed and ruin of our country the length of seven hundred years? I look, and I think I see there is one cause—yes, there is one cause that is there always. It is England, our Enemy. *There* is a nation that would never rest—

never until she had taken away our freedom. The space of half a thousand years she kept our nation in endless strife and shedding of blood because she would not let us live in peace. Thinking that she could conquer us only because she was larger and more numerous she let armies against us, armies upon armies, killing and burning. As if it were not enough, and not to put all her confidence in the chance of battle, she is always watching there, and no opportunity has passed but she has taken it for stirring up and keeping turmoil within this kingdom with the hope to weaken it. All this our nation suffers and endures at her hands, only for the crime of wishing to live in freedom.

"But all that she can do is nothing. Every generation, although it may be torn and battered and covered with the wounds of her invasions, is able to pass to those that come after their liberty at least. And so at last she, the Enemy, understands that our nation is never to be conquered by armies and invasions. Now she is more subtle, for Cunning is her name. Now she comes with feigned friendship; and with lying promises and gold for our traitors she is able to obtain it, and our liberty is at an end!

"But will she yet leave us in peace? No, never! Because we will not have the uncouth German creature we rise once, and again once, for our freedom and our king. At last she wins a battle. God save every nation from knowing England a Victor! What do I see! Our Albannaich won many battles, but no man that was wounded or a prisoner in their hands ever suffered hurt to one hair of his head: they were long marching in the very land of England, where they went as victors, and not a man of the English could say he had suffered from their passing either in his possessions or in his own body;—a thing that was never heard of in war till it was spoken of our countrymen. But neither was there ever heard of among Christian peoples such things as were done as their daily custom by the soldiers of England, victorious in one battle. My father—may he have his share of Paradise! —had but one hand, one hand and a stump. He was not yet four years old the day the red soldier cut off his fingers with a blow of his sword. But the rest that could be told about that it is a shame even to mention. . . . The end of all is that our nation is helpless. England now takes our men to kill them in distant countries fighting in her quarrels. Us also who remain she governs at her will."

Here he paused; then went on.

"But is it yet the end? The end that that nation, England, was pursuing those seven hundred years was the conquest of Alba; and not alone the taking away of our liberty, but our destruction as a people (for until we are destroyed as a people we will rise again). But when can such an end be said to be consummated? Not surely as long as Albannaich remain, who are Albannaich not in name only but who know and feel themselves to be Albannaich, who live in the land after the ways of the forefathers and speak their language. Then, will not England go on now and not be satisfied till all such are wiped out? since till then she is not safe, her conquest is not complete. And if so is not this that is threatening us, our destruction, a part and incident of that conquest?

"Maybe you laugh at that, Maighstir Sachairi . . . maybe you say it is going a long way about to come by a very near-hand thing. Maybe you say it is only a question of greed, the greed of Mac 'Ic Eachainn and the Black Foreigner, and the Black Foreigner's hatred of us and our language; and not a question of our Enemy at all. Greed it is certainly, and hatred; and *yet* it may be a part of that conquest.

"For consider . . . Conquest is not only a matter of defeats in battle. If a nation gives up its ways and its language and the things that belong to its nationality, and takes the ways and language of another nation, then it can be said to have been conquered by that other nation. No matter whether it was defeated in battle or not. And if some men in a nation take on the ways and language of another nation, having given up those that belong to themselves, then they have in a true sense been conquered by that other nation, even though they still remain subjects within their own. *But they*

will be dangerous subjects to their liberties. How was it so
easy for England since the beginning to find those who
would take her gold to raise tumult in the kingdom? and to
lead the Albannaich treacherously to give her victory? How
was it possible for England that time to get our Parliament
so easily to sign away the freedom of their country which
their forefathers had valued above everything and always
given their lives to preserve? Why were traitors so many in
a nation so devoted to freedom? It was because there had
begun to be amongst us those that were not altogether
Albannaich for they had forgotten the language of the forefathers and taken on an English language, with English
ways. Now a man who speaks English and is English in his
ways will begin to feel like those whose language he speaks,
and it is his own countrymen that will seem like foreigners
to him, for their ways are strange and he does not understand their language. And so it was easy for them to be
traitors and betray the nation's liberties, for as they themselves were already English in a certain sort it became much
less easy for them to see good reason why they should not
also be subjects of England, more especially if they could
profit by it. So when the chance offered they lightly sold the
liberties that for them were now valueless. If they had been
Albannaich, true Albannaich, who had never forgotten our
language and the ways of our forefathers, they would not
have sold those liberties for their lives, for they would have
known that to be English and the subjects of England was
for them the same thing as to cease to be.

"But this is what I wish to say . . . If a man speaks an
English language and his ways are English ways, then to his
fellow-countrymen who are still truly Albannaich he will be
just the same as a true Englishman; he will be bound to act
upon the body of his fellow-countrymen who are still
Albannaich exactly as if he were sent by England to be an
agent of her conquest. And that whether he knows it and
means to do it or not. Only because he speaks the foreign
language he will be forcing the Albannaich to learn and use
it, and by so doing to forget their own; and he will influence

them to take on his ways, which are English ways;—and
so without knowing it he is accomplishing in his measure the
very thing that England was trying to bring about when she
invaded us with armies. It is the same conquest, only the
manner of it is different.

" But—and this is it now—all will not be as passive as
the man who only speaks the foreign language and is foreign
in his ways. It is a thing I have noticed myself about a great
number of men, that whatever is strange to them, or whatever
they do not understand, that they hate. And what a man
hates it is natural he will act against; and if he can he will
put it out of the world. It seems, and it is our great misfortune, that the Factor is such a man. He hates us—he says
it himself—and therefore intends to destroy us. But if he
hates us—this too he admits openly—it is only because on
account of our ways and our language we are altogether
something outside his understanding; for he is a foreigner,
although he be of our nation. And so he hates us and will
destroy us, for being Albannaich.

" It is not otherwise with Mac 'Ic Eachainn. You may say
it is his greed. But since the Parliament of England took
away the land from us and gave it to Mac 'Ic Eachainn
there have been three that were Mac 'Ic Eachainn, and the
first of them was as greedy a man as you might find any-
where. It was in his power too to have done this, but if it
would have profited him twice as much I believe he could
not have done it, for he was one man among us like ourselves, of our nation and language; we had upheld him, even
in the field, and to do such a thing to us would have been
like murdering his own father. I am not saying that a man
will never afflict those of his own race and language, or
that only foreigners are tyrants; nevertheless it seems quite
certain that the more a man is aware in himself that he is
a member with others in the one folk and nation the more
he will restrain towards those others the worst excesses of
his greed and selfishness. Mac 'Ic Eachainn is greedy because
it is in his nature to be greedy; so was it in his grandfather's
nature. But Mac 'Ic Eachainn lets his greed make him an

oppressor and our destroyer because he was brought up to be a foreigner, and is not aware within himself that he has part with us or ought to have care over us. To him we are no more than a strange and foreign people and it is nothing to him that it is our livelihood and our very lives that are between him and the satisfaction of his greed. Thus those Albannaich that become like the foreigners are turned, many of them, into haters of their own people, and when the occasion offers to profit them they will destroy and exterminate them after the very fashion of invaders and conquerers.

"It means that Mac 'Ic Eachainn and the Black Factor as well as all that have deserted the things of our nation are, among us, the same as an English army occupying our country. It does not matter whether they know or do not know that they have taken sides with the old Enemy of our freedom and are acting as agents of her conquest; for us, Albannaich, who suffer from it, it only matters that we are being conquered. Yesterday Gleann Mór and Srath Meadhonach were of our nation, held and inhabited by men who were Albannaich: to-day they are desolate only for a few foreigners speaking in the English tongue. A man who has seen conquests can tell if this is not a conquest.

"England does not now lead armies against us, Maighstir Sachairi. She has no need; she only sits at her ease, waiting till the Albannaich that have forgotten to be Albannaich, her allies without knowing it, have accomplished for her the work of her conquest. But she is watching it, she will not let them be resisted till the work is finished—for as we saw at Dùn Eachainn she is prompt whenever need be to come to their help with her law and government, and in the name of Law and Government. The day she looks for—and it is coming near, and this thing will hasten it—is the day there will be Albannaich no longer who speak our language or remember the way of the forefathers and the things that belong to their nation: for that day she will have our country, we can never rise again. At the end of so long a time Alba will not be. The world will be, and nations: but *our* nation will not be."

The Poet sat as he had been speaking.

When the silence went beyond what might have followed naturally the conclusion of his speech, he seemed to listen. . . . He did not turn his head.

When there still was silence an inertness seemed to overcome his attitude; he seemed to droop. At last he spoke again. And it was as if he had abandoned reasons and positions, everything, in one final supplication, directly to the person.

" Maighstir Sachairi, do you not think this ought to be resisted? "

Still he did not look at Maighstir Sachairi. No doubt he feared to look.

3

If he had looked he would have been surprised and more than surprised, for what he would have seen was one thing he could never have anticipated. . . .

In the time he had been speaking, and all unknown to him as he reasoned and laboured to be more clear than reason, Maighstir Sachairi had undergone, and emerged from, such an experience as seemed to him undergoing it to be more profound and core-reaching, of more moment in his soul and spirit, if it were possible, even than his conversion itself.

It would not be true to say that this was occasioned by anything Fearchar the Poet said. Maighstir Sachairi's mind by the direction given to it even in infancy, as well as by his later training and long discipline, was able to act only (as it were) on the vertical plane: he thought of ' *God*,' and ' *man* ' or ' *men*,' and understood events only as produced in the tensions between the Divine and human wills; and not otherwise was he able to understand the world. Hence he was unable to think historically, for that is as it were horizontally; incapable from the very nature of his mind of recognising the validity of a view which might seek to explain events as the product of factors working out in a process that must be called historical. In effect, Fearchar's reasoning swayed him not at all, for it followed a line which led it always outside his accustomed categories. He could not see that there might be causes other than what might be called theological for the act of this destruction; no more could he see that destruction as an event which would itself enter into the process of history and let loose a train of others leading of necessity, if unprevented, to an end that was predictable.

Nevertheless although the old man's reasoning had been without persuasion it was not unconnected with the experience that seemed to Maighstir Sachairi so momentous; and was in fact the occasion of it.

The peculiar ailment, or disorder of the nerves, or whatever the malady was from which Maighstir Sachairi had been suffering, seemed to exhaust itself or be burnt out in that final moment when it overcame him in a crisis of ungovernable excitement. That crisis left him in a state of death-like exhaustion. He lay rather than sat in the Poet's chair in an almost total intermission of his powers and faculties, for had he been able to realise it, it was only that now-vanished excitement and fever of the mind that had upheld him in an almost constant activity during the long period when, though hardly aware of it, he had scarcely slept or eaten. He sat therefore in his dwam, and took refuge behind the Poet's speaking till he should regain possession of himself.

It was not long before there came recovery. But a strange recovery. For while he shortly found his mind returning to him clear and calm, purged of agitation and the confusion that had lately clouded it, his body remained submerged under the same wave of exhaustion that had first overwhelmed body and mind together. Perhaps from that very circumstance—that his body remained sunk and drowned in an unconsciousness of extreme exhaustion—his mind had its unwonted clarity and calm; for thus it was not distracted or drawn downwards, as is normal with us, by matter.

Instead in that moment he experienced an extraordinary lightness and airy freedom, as if he were disembodied and had become pure spirit, a separated and free intelligence.

With this calm and clear mind he began at once to give attention to the Poet;—since to a disembodied, pure intelligence there is nothing left but *to understand,* and it must at once seek an object in order to unite itself with it in an act of understanding, such an act being the sole end of its nature. Moreover with his mind's unwonted calm and freedom there came a strange anticipation, like an intimation of things about to be understood that had been inaccessible while his body clogged him.

The Poet was still at the beginning of his long argument, warming to it. On his brow and over his cheek-bones the colour came and went. His eyes looked straight before him, but saw only the things he spoke of, passing in his mind; they were sombre, then sad, and now a glint of indignation lighted them. Now and again his nostrils quivered. His light voice which in its normal tones was soft and even-sounding had taken a note from his intensity; it spoke for him and for his case as eloquently as did his words; starting away, and pausing, demanding, and replying, now vibrant in slow ascending indignation, dropping down then on a note of heart-break, continuing a long space in even reasonableness; so *alive* that more than once it seemed to reside apart in its own intensity and to be speaking from itself.

Maighstir Sachairi took note of all this, perceiving the Poet's earnestness. And perceiving that, he was all at once aware of something he had never formerly understood, and had even many times denied; namely that a man might refuse his doctrine, might be given up to carnal courses, devoted to vanities, a servant of the world and the own affections of his fleshly mind—and yet sincere in all, and of a good conscience. Not a liar or hypocrite, nor wilfully shutting his eyes to the truth. He looked at Fearchar, and found it difficult to believe, now, that he had *hated* this man, as a wilful evildoer and conscious servant of the Devil; that the sight of his small graceful figure, his fine head, his flow-ing beard, had once moved him to intense dislike; that he even—he almost chuckled—used to think to himself that inside his boot his twisted foot must resemble, if indeed it was not in fact and in reality, a hoof, and cloven. Looking at Fearchar now, the fire shining in him; hearing the voice, charged with his poet's fervour till the lowest tones of it touched the ear with an instant persuasion; he thought him at that moment in his fervour and old age, beautiful. He was moved to admiration of his one-time enemy. What sincerity! he thought. His honesty is through and through him! It is as if not his voice is speaking but he himself, his very being! Maighstir Sachairi was suddenly filled full with this admiration, seeing the Poet in that instant as all his life a fine and noble spirit, big-natured, sorrowful, alone, and kind, almost heroic. And because this generous wave and impulse came directly from his heart spontaneously and was entirely a movement of his being *outward*, an impresonal act of homage and recognition, and far above self; so it liberated, and was accompanied in his mind by a sense unbelievably heightened of freedom, of an illumination.

A sense almost unbearably heightened. For it happened then. Without pause or anything intermediate his mind achieved that knowledge which had been intimated, the transforming vision in a timeless instant. He understood how Fearchar and he had lived in different universes. He saw that universe that was Fearchar's, the world that was the world as Fearchar saw and felt it, and it had an actuality and clearness that made it eternally true, and for Fearchar. But by no means had he himself passed into it, to live in it henceforward. Far, far from that; for he saw his own world simultaneously and it was true also with an equal actuality.

And not only these universes but the whole life of men, the entire world of their acts in motion, with their sorrows, pains, triumphs, aspirations—all this he seemed to see, as if from above, from outside himself, with detachment and not participation. A vision of all humanity (as it seemed), synoptic, mystical; an instant vision of man's life, but viewed tragically, from the angle of his destiny. The lives of his own people too—*this destruction will take place, inescapably,* he saw that now, as if the veil of the future had been drawn aside for him; but from this serene height he was able to view even that event with calm, for he saw it within the sum of human things, as it were indifferently to the wills of any that were concerned, so that it moved him without moving him. Indeed the impulse of his being was altogether in affirmation; he might have said: All is good! Life is good, and death is good, and all between! Our salvation is good; and our destruction at the oppressor's hand—that is good also. He knew in that moment that his own fate must be bound and compassed there; but he cared not to see it, he only knew that his life must be different now. . . .

Turning again to the Poet and listening to him, seeing him put forth the whole resources of his gifts in this final effort whose success meant everything to him, he began to say to himself, Poor Fearchar! poor Fearchar! He did not know why he said this. He might have interrupted, for no argument mattered now. But seeing him in full course he felt the brutality it would be to stop him. So he sat looking at him, feeling an inexplicable warmth about his eyes, saying to himself, Poor Fearchar! poor Fearchar! He began listening to the words, noting their force, tenfold increased said as the Poet said them. He was well content to sit there listening. He began to follow the argument and was moved to a quiet enthusiasm of admiration. How true that it as you argue it! he thought. And, O Poet!

So when the old man finished speaking he was ready to strike his hands together for admiration. In the silence that followed he was smiling at Fearchar appraisingly and with a kind of pride in him.

At length drawing a long breath and shaking his head slowly he said in a kind of smiling sorrow, " O Fearchar, Fearchar! . . . that head you have! . . . your eloquence! . . . What a pity you served the wrong Master! "

At the first word the old man bowed his head and groaned aloud.

Maighstir Sachairi sat looking at him compassionately, with a thoughtful, kind smile.

"Fearchar," he said after a while in a gentle voice, smiling still, and with a note of gentle banter, "Fearchar, do you know what I am to tell you? I am going to tell you the truth about yourself. For I have found you out. It is not a Christian that is in you at all, but a pagan or papist."

Fearchar turned round a face of amazement. Meeting the minister's gentle, indulgent smile he was disconcerted. But all at once he became offended at that smile. He flushed, and when he spoke it was in a rather sharp tone, and with a look of irritation. "Which of the two am I then, Maighstir Sachairi, pagan or papist? Or can I be both at once?"

"Oh, yes, indeed, Fearchar. For they are the same in this," said Maighstir Sachairi, pushing himself up a little in the chair by his elbows and still smiling his kindly smile and not seeming to have noticed Fearchar's irritation.

"You see, Fearchar, the saints, Christians, are saved out of the world, rapt away out of the world as it were, though we still continue to live in it for the period of our lives here below. But we have no portion here. And so neither the world itself nor any of its affairs is our concern, not even the things of nations and governments and rulers, unless it should happen that they touch the Will of God, or the carrying out of His Judgments, or the spreading of His Kingdom. If tyrants and the ungodly, not as the agents of God's Judgments but of their own will and from greed or hatred, oppress the people of God, to bring ruin upon them and scatter them, then it would be right certainly to resist them. Or again if God's people in a nation can take into their hands the government of that nation and become its rulers, so as to put down the ungodly and unbelievers and bind the truth and the law of God if need be by force upon all, then too they would be right in so doing, for it would be spreading the Kingdom. But to resist God's chastisements only because they are bitter, though the agents of them may be tyrants, that would be to add sin to sin. Or to take to do with governments and rulers simply so that things may be thus and thus between nations, or that such and such a way of life may be kept up because it is the old way and seems good in our eyes, or so that such and such another way of life may be cast out because it is not natural to us and would make us other than we are in our human likenesses as men in this world: to take to do with such things is not for us as the people of God. (Indeed it might even be gravely wrong; for an earthly government, if it cherishes the people of God and defends His church and does not suffer the idolater, is due our reverent submission in every event, even were it to overthrow the ways of the ages and, removing places, to let in the stranger and the alien; since all authority is from God and it is written that he that resists the power resists the ordinance of God and purchases to himself damnation). With these, therefore, we have nothing to do, because all such things—nations in their dealings with nations, the taking of new ways of life or the keeping of the ways of the forefathers—all these, just like your poetry and your music, Fearchar, belong to man's life on this earth, to the temporal order of this world which is to pass away. And therefore they are worthless things to us upon whom has come the apocalypse of Christ in the soul through Faith. It is for papists and unbelievers to concern themselves and be busy about all such things, for it is they in their darkness who value the natural man and his life and seek after a reasonable good on this earth and a natural justice in the passing world. But the Chosen of God have been converted from the world and the life of fallen man on earth, and can cherish nothing here. They have no time: for they do not look for the salvation of nations *in* the world, but have been saved *out of* the world, and instantly await the Bridegroom's Coming, having their loins girt and their staff in their hand, since it is written that His time none can know, but that He comes in a moment, in the twinkling of an eye."

The Poet had a hand on each knee and was keeping a look of intelligence and understanding mingled with a surprised enlightenment fixed on Maighstir Sachairi while he was speaking, and for a time after he had finished.

"Then," he said, half in question, "it must be bad for a nation when its people become converted to that Faith. While they save their souls, their enemies will have their way with them in this world."

Maighstir Sachairi nodded his head. "It might be even so," he said with his gentle smile. "But it would be so small a loss, and so great a gain!"

Fearchar turned away and sat frowning aside, knitting his brows. He appeared at a loss. Yet he looked dejected too. Absentmindedly he put up the end of his beard to his mouth and sat biting it, with his strong teeth. He made a movement as if shaking something off his shoulders. Then took his hand from his beard and brought it down sharply on his knee. As he did so he flushed.

All at once he was looking at Maighstir Sachairi again and his brow had darkened with anger. "Then, Maighstir Sachairi," he said in a voice that rang with resentment, his blue eyes gleaming fiercely out under the thick white brows, "I must ask you—whose way is better for the people? Would this have been let happen if they were in the same spirit they had when I was their leader? They were as bold as lions until they got this religion. You have made them entirely dependent on you, so that without you they are helpless. You took the leadership out of my hands. Can your way save them now? God be my witness I would rather they were pagans—aye, even papists—if as you say they would thereby strike more deeply with their roots and be more firmly set to preserve our race in its variety and potency on earth! What use is a religion that bids us tear out our bowels in the here and now of our life for the sake of a heaven where also our humanity will be worthless and covered up, and from which after all we may have been shut out by the decree of God before our birth! A fart for such a faith: a people that got it would be destroyed by it: the Devil must have made it!"

But his passion fell from him as quickly as it had risen. Almost without pausing he continued, "I sincerely ask your pardon, Maighstir Sachairi." He bowed his head, and resting his brow against his palm, pressed it there, slowly moving his head from side to side in the gesture of the last abandonment.

Maighstir Sachairi regarded him with pity. He knew it was no small despair.

After a little he began to address him.

"Fearchar, when I came to Gleann Luachrach the great part of the people here were living sinfully. I do not mean by that that great sins and crimes were common amongst them—men were not murdering each other, and adultery and the like were scarcely even heard of. But in their lives they were altogether given over to vanity, and there was scarcely one among them that minded heavenly things. Now there is no doubt that you were the leader in all this. Certainly you had not taught the people this way of life— it was the way of the forefathers, godless men. But being born in it, and finding it around you, I suppose that you threw yourself into those vanities from a boy, and because of your talents you excelled in them; so that when I came to Gleann Luachrach you were like a king and leader. So it had to be that I was your enemy. . . . "

He seemed to break off, and in a different tone went on— "Fearchar, I am going to say something now that will surprise you. I am going to ask your pardon. I am very serious. . . . I want you to forgive me."

The old man took his hand from his head and looked up.

"For what are you asking my pardon, Maighstir Sachairi?"

Maighstir Sachairi did not reply at once. Then he said, seeming to hesitate, "I might say that it is because I was hard and unjust to you . . . Or because I have made you an exile for twenty years in your own place and among your own people . . . Or because for so long I attributed your gifts secretly in my mind to Satan. But I am aware in myself that it is not for all this that I want you to forgive me. Or maybe rather it *is* for all this, but for so much more also that these things, or any particular things, do not matter at all. . . . I will simply speak it as I feel it, Fearchar—I ask your pardon for . . . *for everything.*"

The Poet had his eyes fixed on the minister, trying to understand. For a moment, noting how Maighstir Sachairi's eyes were shining, it occurred to him that he might still be ill or in a fever. But he dismissed the thought. He understood that something had happened to Maighstir Sachairi—some experience—and that he was meaning something when he spoke like that.

He said, puzzled, " You have surprised me, Maighstir Sachairi. . . . But you have no right to ask my pardon now. I thought at that time—and I still think it—that your way was wrong. But I never bore you a grudge. On the contrary I respected you. I would not have respected you if you had done otherwise, seeing the matter as I knew you saw it. . . . But, forgive me, you have no right to ask my pardon unless you have come to my way of thinking."

" You are wrong, Fearchar. I both have the right to ask your pardon and I *ought* to ask it—yours and everybody's. Yes, I was right then to do as I did; were it now I suppose I would do it again. Yet I ought to ask your pardon."

The Poet turned away, and fell to stroking his long beard. There is something strange in him, he thought. What can he mean? and why does he look so strangely? He is like a man that has been visited. . . .

Finally he said, " I am very willing to forgive you, Maighstir Sachairi—if only I understand you and have anything to forgive you for! Only bear with me once more—let me point out to you how you have already saved us from the destruction of Gleann Mór and Srath Meadhonach. . . . "

He was going to continue but Maighstir Sachairi interrupted; and by his voice Fearchar thought he was smiling again. In fact Maighstir Sachairi had smiled when he heard him speak, although not humorously, but rather with a faint smile of recognition.

He said, " I know what you are going to say, Fearchar. I have had it argued to me before, and it is no discredit to you that he argued it even better than you could. This was how he spoke:— It is every man's duty if he can to prevent sin and evil, (and it your duty more especially as you are a minister of Christ). But violence and destruction are sin and evil: they are a sin in those who do them and an evil to those who suffer them. Therefore it is no less than your duty to oppose the Factor, for by doing so you both prevent him from committing a sin and save the people of this glen from as great an evil as could befall them in the world. And then he pointed me, as you did, to Srath Meadhonach and Gleann Mór, saying:— That only happened because the people there had no one to protect them, and the Factor has committed a great sin for which God will punish him only because no one would save him by preventing him. But— he said—in Gleann Luachrach the people still have their homes and possessions, and that is only because you once outfaced the Factor and threatened to oppose him. That was therefore a good act—he argued—since it prevented evil and suffering. And surely—(he said this many times, he seemed to think it a strong argument)—surely it is a good and praiseworthy thing that by an act of yours a man will stand before his God with one great sin the less that he must answer for. And then he was fond of saying (thinking I would not notice he flattered my vanity):— It is not only a good act and your duty to oppose the Factor in this, but it will even be easy, for you are far stronger than the Factor, one word of yours and he will never dare to lift his hand."

The old man had been staring at the minister as if he could scarcely believe his ears. He said, incredulously, " *Who* argued like this? "

Maighstir Sachairi smiled. He leaned a little forward and dropping his voice almost to a whisper, pronounced the one word—" *Satan*! "

The Poet looked at him a moment and without a word turned away. In a minute he turned towards him again. " I cannot understand it, Maighstir Sachairi. You say yourself that God has put this people in your charge so that you should have care over them and protect them. Yet when destruction threatens you give way to the oppressor. I cannot understand it. They are the brethren of Christ, Maighstir Sachairi. And when you do not protect them it seems to me—forgive me speaking plainly—that you are doing the same thing as Peter did when he three times denied the Lord."

Maighstir Sachairi shook his head slowly from side to side, as if to say it was too late to go into all that again.

"It is between my soul and God," he said.

"But it is ruin for *us*," added Fearchar.

He sat for a long time resting his elbow on his knee, and his head against his hand, so that his face was hidden.

Maighstir Sachairi was as calm now, as quiet and patient, as he had earlier been agitated. From that moment of vision and affirmation he maintained a reality of his being which could not be beaten upon and diminished by outside things; so that however long the silence might have lasted it could never have embarrassed him. Whether he broke it or Fearchar, or whether it continued, was of serene indifference, for there was no longer in him anything of *wanting*, or haste or impatience. But when he had sat for a long time so, he addressed Fearchar. "Did you say that you never bore me a grudge, Fearchar?—never?"

The Poet stirred. "No," he said, but in such a tone as made it doubtful if the meaning of the question had yet reached him through his brooding, "No, Maighstir Sachairi, I never bore you a grudge."

In a moment he spoke again. "Well, maybe, to be altogether honest. . . . Yes, maybe I did bear you a grudge, Maighstir Sachairi. Once. For one thing!"

"What thing was that, Fearchar?"

"It was the papers, Maighstir Sachairi."

Maighstir Sachairi's eyes clouded, then lightened. "I remember!"

After a little—"The papers, Fearchar. . . . I remember that you valued them greatly. They were poems and the like, I know;—but what was in them exactly? Where did they come from at the first?"

The Poet looked round and looked away. "They came out of Dùn Eachainn, Maighstir Sachairi. Since you ask it I will tell you." His blue eyes were sombre now. His air had become that of a man who bore a hard thing with dignity, it was even a little distant, though without offence.

"About twenty years ago there was great building at Dùn Eachainn. You will remember it, for it was about the time you came to Gleann Luachrach. Mac 'Ic Eachainn had died the year before, and Mac 'Ic Eachainn was making his house as big as it is now. There was an old part at the east side, the oldest part of the house, and they pulled it down. And in the wall they found the box and the papers in it. Domhnall Mór mac Thomais found it—Mac-Amhlaidh, the father of Domhnall Gorm—he was a mason and was working there. It seems he took it to Mac 'Ic Eachainn, and I don't know if he hoped to get a reward or not but Mac 'Ic Eachainn only looked and saw the writing was in the Gaelic language and told him to take it away and not trouble him. Domhnall was to throw the papers away for he could not read himself, but for some reason instead of that he brought them home. Well, it happened there was some tailor going about in the glen at that time who was said to be a notable teller of tales, and one night when he happened to be in Domhnall's house I myself went down there. And I found the tailor using the first of the papers for shapes for a garment he was making for Domhnall mac Thomais. That was how they came to be mine; for I bought them from Domhnall that evening."

"And what was in them exactly, Fearchar?"

"Well then it must have been a very long time since the man hid them in the wall at Dùn Eachainn, and no doubt many were old even before then, and some of them you could hardly read at all because of their age. And they were all in a very old Gaelic that nobody speaks nowadays. But the great-part of them I made out to be concerned with the history of this neighbourhood and the family of Mac 'Ic Eachainn, and these were written by a certain Domhnall Mór MacEoin and Domhnall Og MacEoin—I suppose that Baile MhicEoin would be named from one of them. There were a considerable number of poems, too, and many of them I myself was able to read after I had studied them. I do not know who made these, but he was a scholarly and cultivated poet, and not an unlearned bard such as I."

"And those I took away from you and destroyed!" Maighstir Sachairi said. "Forgive me, Fearchar, I see only now that you have very much to forgive me for. I know that being a poet yourself and a seanchaidh you must have greatly valued the papers. And I would have been surprised indeed if you had not borne me a grudge."

The old man made no reply.

All at once he was speaking again. "I . . . I am afraid I have not been quite open with you, Maighstir Sachairi. I have not told you of the greater part of my resentment and what it came from. It was because . . . I don't know how you will take my saying it . . . well, it was because I felt you were a poet yourself . . . I felt . . . I felt you had *betrayed* us both."

Maighstir Sachairi sat straight up, a look of astonishment on his face. When he spoke, however, he was smiling— "How did you know that? Verily you are a most notable man, Fearchar. What would make you think I once made poems?"

"I did not know if you ever made a poem, Maighstir Sachairi. I only knew you had the poet's mind."

"But how could that be? How did you know that?"

Fearchar gave a faint shrug, looking reflectively at the fire. "I knew it," he said simply.

Maighstir Sachairi waited a little for him to say more. Then he leant back again in the chair. "Yes, it is true," he said in a tone of reminiscence. "There was a time when I was very busy about those vanities—many years ago. I thought I had put it all behind me, but a little while ago I saw that it was still with me without my knowing. The old nature does not die easily, Fearchar, and Satan is very subtle."

A little later glancing at the Poet he noticed the reflection of the fire leaping up and down in his eyes, and only then realised that the dusk was in the room: the sun must have set. In some surprise he rose. But his knees were weak and they trembled under him so that he swayed and staggering clutched the chair.

The Poet noticed it, he too getting up. He said, " Maighstir Sachairi, you refused the dram when you came in. I will offer it again, for I see that truly you are not well."

" I did wrong to refuse, Fearchar," said Maighstir Sachairi turning on him his kindly smile. " Forgive me again. Yes, I will take the dram with pleasure."

Standing with the glass in his hand he removed his bonnet; and Fearchar did likewise, bowing his head. " May God let nothing to our bodies that will harm our souls! " the minister said, and took the dram. " Amen! " said the old man fervently.

Maighstir Sachairi moved to the door. " Oh, for God's sake, Maighstir Sachairi "—the words broke from Fearchar —" be merciful! Have pity on them! "

Maighstir Sachairi turned with his hand on the door latch. He looked at the bowed head of the old man and compassion and a great sadness came to his eyes.

" Believe me, Fearchar,"—his voice trembled—" I pity them from the bottom of my heart."

He opened the door.

A gentle rain had for a long time been falling noiselessly. A faint wind of evening came in and fluttered over him, fresh and cool, smelling sweetly of the bedewed earth.

He looked down the glen.

Night was descending.

CHAPTER EIGHT

MAIGHSTIR SACHAIRI came out of his house and walked towards the church. He carried his bible under his arm, walking slowly.

The first clang of the bell—struck, dropped in the pool of Sabbath quiet. Sang out on widening circles in the air, more melodious more diminishing. And struck. . . .

The vision that he had in the house of the Poet, had left him, and was with him still, with him now. It had left him, for that it did not seem to be a thing in time, but was as if his consciousness—bound along the line of extending time —passed among the others in succession one single moment of so thin a surface that the light of the eternal, penetrating, lit it up within: it was a timeless vision, therefore, for as it was something seen in a moment of eternity's breaking in, it was outside the continuous and could not know it. But because eternity, lighting a moment, lights in that present all time both past and yet to some, so all his days since then had been lighted in that single Simultaneous: which, so, remained with him.

At least, with the same strange calm he had ever since continued to see the world, and events past, and the thing that was to be. Not that he was unmoved by this last, or forgetful. Day and night it stood before his mind, and perhaps it had never seemed more awful or more profoundly moved him. It so moved him that all the torments he had suffered formerly, thinking of it, appeared as nothing to what he suffered now. The time was long past (long past, as it seemed) when the glen's destruction revolted him because it was wanton and meaningless, an irruption of irrational, irresponsible elements submerging in a wave and triumph of disorder, order and things intelligible. That, (although it was a pain), he had perceived after Mairi-of-Eoghann-Gasda to be no more than the revolt of his mind, his natural mind, and not without Sin. Now it was far otherwise. Deeper. Now it turned in the very bowels of his humanity. What he saw now was its effect on persons, this or that person, man or woman, whom he knew like parts of himself and whose welfare and happiness, it turned out, had been tied with him in his own heart. (This old saintly woman to die of exposure and the violence of her turning out; that young pair to see their life's course together in one day deflected down to pools of troubles, shallows of want; and that other, who had always lived respected in the enjoyment of abundance, to pass his age despised, in poverty, the servant of another). But all that he suffered moved him so, yet without moving him; indeed since that one moment in the Poet's house the more he suffered the more he was not moved, or moved only to acceptance. For in the light of that moment, that Simultaneous, he saw this that was coming and must come *as if it had been already past*. And therefore it could no longer appear before him as something about which he must decide or act. There was hereafter no acting or deciding, not even submission—only aceptance, acceptance. It was no longer something from outside approaching; but something which he had already experienced and was experiencing, interiorly. It was nothing either that he knew his own fate was not elsewhere or in other times or places, but bound to its consummation here. All that was or was to be, whether God smote to the uttermost or in His mercy still spared some, whether he himself died or lived—all that was equal now, all gathered and lifted up together in one, Thy will be done!

On earth as it is in heaven! It was even the cause of a lifting-up and secret inspiration of the mind to reflect upon it thus: himself walking on Earth towards the inevitableness of that Event, which now was *to be*, and then, later, would *have been*—but in Heaven since before the beginning, *is*. Such a realisation, such an intuition of the Simultaneous, both lifted the mind clear above the flow and passing of human affairs so far as to the contemplation of them in removedness, and equal, all; and yet gave to the smallest action now a significance it was never real with formerly. ' Himself walking on the earth '—*he; on Earth;* and *walking.* Eoghann Ogha-Duibhne pulling on the rope made the bell peal out and pealing give the air a pulse of his own vigour, set his manhood a-throb on it. Airy miles over hills, trees, houses, filled with it, filling and ebbing, with the sound, the rhythm. It was now the day, the day now, the Sabbath. . . .

Not only Maighstir Sachairi knew it. For twenty years, from midday of the Sabbath and for two hours and more thereafter, and then again for two hours and more, the great part of Gleann Luachrach had always been in their places, in the kirk. That from their duty, and their sense of it. But recently from fear, and in many cases from a real re-awakened fervour and desire towards God. Who in permitting them to see the face of oppression and danger near them, close at hand, had seen fit to make them know their defence-lessness and the insufficiency of the help that is in man; to remind them Where was their protection. For if their danger came from enemies, God is the protector of the oppressed; but even if from offended God,—where shall a man flee from God's justice but to His mercy! All this time many would have come to the church gladly not on the Sabbath only, when it was open, but every day.

But this Sabbath Gleann Luachrach had set out. Maighstir Sachairi had neither spoken nor acted differently since the night he was in Fearchar the Poet's dwelling. Indeed and on the contrary he appeared to have reverted to his most usual self. He ceased from that night to remain shut up in his own house, God knew how engaged, and if anything was more frequently among them than at any time; and there was nothing now in his words or conduct that could be named as strange. He was calm, his words chosen, and spoken in sobriety, his bearing irreproachably of a minister. Yet if it could not be named, it had been visible to everyone; every man on whom he turned his slow, calm glance experienced a something deeply disturbing, as if it had been a stound of dread or premonition of catastrophe: when he had gone from a house people surprised each other's eyes, and knew that more than they had seen it. And this first Sabbath an entire parish was converging on the church. Single figures and small groups had been for some time coming out of the distance. Getting more numerous. Figures on foot, on horseback, carts jolting along the slopes. Aged people and infirm in them who had considered themselves and been considered to be beyond this journey. When the bell swung out they were moving so blackly on all converging ways that from a distance they seemed twice too numerous for the square building on the knoll. The note of the bell hastened them, swinging out over them with the note of foreboding that sound will always hold when the heart is disquieted.

Maighstir Sachairi saw without remarking it that there were more carts than usual drawn up below the knoll. It was a cool day, the glen bright and green under intensely white glittering cloud masses floating in the blue. A breeze rose from time to time gusting about coolly. The sun was somewhere.

Inside the church was their breathing, that sense and tension that tells without a look that every place is filled. Maighstir Sachairi did not look round, mounting to the pulpit. When he had sat for a little and bowed his head in prayer, he stood. First his calm-in-suffering glance travelled about the walls and ceiling. It's bare here! he thought, seeing the building for the first time, that it was bare and plain. He reflected: a little brightness would have been more fitting here, some colour on those forbidding walls—shapes or figures to take away their bareness! Then he looked calmly at the congregation. His eyes passed over them without haste, row after row. In twenty years of Sabbaths he knew this churchful so well that in one glance he could detect a stranger or newcomer; he saw at once all the infirm and aged that were not usually there. But his eyes moved on, searching the rows. Ah! he was thinking, then he has not forgiven me! Or perhaps his pride still keeps him away . . . .

He looked down at his book and in a strong voice gave out the psalm.

There was a small moving throughout the church. Which died away.

The smith stood up. Looking trim and slimmer washed and in his sabbath dress, a handsome strong man. He coughed and pitched the note, keeping his eyes cast down, his manner betraying some disquiet or nervousness in him to-day. His voice was thin and unsure singing the line. And the congregation joined thinly, many voices, not as usual, remaining silent. Those who sang for the most part sat erect, their eyes lifted above the heads of the congregation, looking straight before them. In the second line the smith sang more surely, his single tenor rising clearly; the feeling that came from his disquiet was in his singing now. And after him the people joined more numerously. Then it was: *Moladh gach ni an taobh stigh dhiom 'Ainm naomha mar is còir—and suddenly the smith was singing as he could sing; and the congregation had taken it up with loud and certain voice. O my soul bless thou now Great Jehovah thy God. . . . As if all the misgivings of their hearts suddenly found relief and outflowed in praising Him their God and their hope, so they sang now. Loud, loud. Loud and clear the clear rich tenor sang alone. The building filled with the voice of the people soaring, singing. . . . O forget not the benefits the Lord has vouchsafed to thee! . . . A fervour caught them in the crowded church, being troubled inwardly and disquieted. The building was filled, charged with it.

Only Maighstir Sachairi remained strangely outside it; praying, and when he read the chapter. His voice rose as ever and went out to every corner of the church, strong, with a faint chill at the core of its resonance. He seemed remote and apart in some calm, cold fervour of his own. Different.

The text. . . .

In the Book of Deuteronomy, and in the eighth chapter—" And thou shalt remember all the way which the Lord thy

*Praise all that is within me His Holy Name as is just.

God led thee these forty years in the wilderness, to humble thee, and to prove thee, and to know what was in thy heart, whether thou wouldst keep his commandments or no. He humbled thee and suffered thee to hunger that he might make thee know that man doth not live by bread only, but by every word that proceedeth out of the mouth of the Lord doth man live." And again—" God, Who led thee through the great and terrible wilderness, that he might humble thee, and that he might prove thee, to do thee good at thy latter end."

He closed the book.

To not a few, being fearful, that had sounded already a sufficiently notable text, and of bitter application. Their heads were bowed; or else they sat looking at the minister in a kind of paralysis of anticipation, of apprehension, unable not to watch his lips. There was a rustling of clothes throughout the church and in different parts a subdued coughing; the people settling themselves to listen. Then, silence.

But about the time when the minister's voice should have been heard in his opening words there was no sound. The silence lengthened. Some glanced up towards the pulpit where the minister was standing very erect, looking at them. The same rustling and subdued coughing got up again, and gradually died away once more into silence. They waited. . .

Now all over the church people were staring up at the pulpit. More and more eyes were drawn to look and became fixed there. Something was happening. The minister was staring down at them with a terrifying aspect, his grey hair framing the stricken face. He seemed to be undergoing some fearful struggle inside himself; his lips moved as if in speech. Then, his voice was heard—if it was his voice. A high, broken gabble of words that stopped abruptly. Only those nearest caught some words of it—" the way the Lord thy God led thee. . . . " It was his text that he had tried to repeat. He stared down at them, gripping the pulpit.

Consternation seized their hearts. Women cast fearful glances aside at husbands, who ignored the looks, rigidly maintaining a proper bearing; and with blenched faces.

Then—The minister had sat down. A quick gasp went up from the congregation, and was instantly checked into silence. They waited still. . . .

Suddenly, the whole church had broken out in movement. A sound had come from the pulpit, in the deathly silence every person in the church had heard it. A *sob*. The building was filled with a rustling and turning, people turning about, looking at each other in horror. Then this also subsided into a shocked silence. . . .

The miller was first to recover the power to act. He got up from his seat near the front and came walking down the middle of the church, between the rows. His face was deathly pale, his mouth twitching. He kept his eyes on the ground. With his arm he was supporting Gilleasbuig Liath who hobbled and staggered, making a clattering noise with his stick on the floor. The congregation, sitting in their places, turned their heads slowly, in a kind of fascination following their progress to the door.

They had almost reached the door when a number got to their feet in different parts of the church. Others then. In a moment the whole people were up and pressing in silence out of the church. Turning white faces over their shoulders to cast fearful glances at the huddled and motionless figure in the pulpit.

2

Presuming on his privilege as the minister's 'man' Lachlan MacMhuirich slipped past the pulpit and came out at a small door that led to the vestry. Emerging he cast one glance over his shoulder as if to see that he was not observed, and hurried across with his awkward gait and went into the stable.

He closed both the top and the lower portions of the door behind him quickly, and stood still in the sudden dusk. For a while he stood still there, chin in hand. The horse had looked round when he came in, and seeing him went back to its munching. But as Lachlan MacMhuirich remained stand-

ing there without moving the munching noise became slower
and less rhythmical, and stopped now and then. Then it
stopped altogether. The animal turned its head, showing the
whites of its eyes, and looked at him. It whinnied softly and
began moving its feet. Lachlan MacMhuirich leant and put
his ear to the door, listening. Hearing nothing he went over
and stood craning his neck to see if he could see through
the one little square of window. It was covered with cobwebs,
old spiders' webs full of dust and with flies' wings and dry
fly-corpses hanging. He returned to the door and cautiously
opened the upper portion far enough to apply an ear; his
good eye, too, was peeping out occasionally. First he heard,
close by though out of sight, a long procession passing on
the track above him. Intermittent noises, harness jingling, a
wheel creaking, a hoof clinked against a stone. These were
going up the glen. They were passing in complete silence.
Several times it seemed that all had passed, then there came
to the ear again a succession of small noises of movement.
Someone coughed, a man cleared his throat—the noise was
close, it startled. This passing went on for a long time. Then
followed silence. Long afterwards small black figures appeared on the distant slope of the glen, moving singly or in
groups, scattering towards the houses. Lachlan MacMhuirich
withdrew his head and closed the door. He climbed the
ladder to the loft above the stable and went stooping because
of the lowness of the rafters and lay down on his bed.

Hours passed. The sun dipped down towards the west.
He was so motionless that he might have been asleep, lying
there. But his eyes were wide open, staring up at the rafters.
Outside the day was fine, the small pane among the slates
showed a light blue square of sky. Which became white
from time to time, then blue again. The fresh wind rose
occasionally to a gust in which the slates rattled faintly. In
the stable below a bluefly was buzzing in the beam of sunlight that must be coming through the window, and the
horse could be heard champing and moving its feet.

Gradually shadows were in the loft and the pale square in
the roof began to darken. The shapes of the rafters became

indistinct and sinking back mingled with the shadows. Lachlan MacMhuirich moved. He got up and lit a candle, then sat on the edge of the bed with his hands between his knees. Several times he cleared his throat involuntarily. The candle sitting near the floor was blown upon by various draughts of air and sent the shadows frog-leaping fantastically. After a time Lachlan MacMhuirich rose, went down and looked to the horse, and returning blew out the candle and lay down on the bed in his former posture, his eye staring up into the darkness. The stars came out.

At last after some hours he moved once more and got up from the bed. This time he settled his bonnet on his head and clambered down the ladder into the stable. He opened the door carefully, went out, and closed it behind him. The night was clear, moonless, but bright with stars. And a cool wind getting up strongly from the east. He stood a while where he was, peering up at the sky, to see by the position of the stars in it that the Sabbath must for certain be over. . . . It was time to do what was to be done.

The back door of the manse was standing ajar. He stood long listening carefully into the house. Hearing nothing he pressed the door gently and stooping, stepping carefully, disappeared inside. Shortly he re-emerged, listening over his shoulder, pulling the door slowly till it was all but closed. Then he set his face eastwards. The hours till dawn were too few, and there were fifteen miles before him. . . .

With his awkward-looking but in reality extremely rapid walk he had accomplished it in little more than three hours. He was standing in the dark tapping urgently at a low window. The window opened a little and stooping he carried on a conversation in urgent whispers with someone inside, a woman. The window closed. Shortly there began a rattling of bolts behind the door, a lock shot back. The door was held open and Lachlan MacMhuirich went hurriedly inside.

The old woman brought two candles and set them in the room. She was in a nightcap, wakened out of her sleep, and went about it sleepily. Going out and closing the door she eyed the man inquisitively.

Lachlan MacMhuirich stood in the room looking about him. There was a massive table with papers scattered about it, and some pens lying. An entire wall occupied to half its height with tiers of drawers and pigeonholes with more papers. Bookcases containing heavy volumes. Lachlan Cearbach seemed uncomfortable and looked about rather furtively. His gaze happening to travel towards the massive fireplace he drew back a step with a quick catching of his breath. He had not noticed a large mirror above the fireplace, and looking in that direction—the table with the candles being in front of him—had all at once been startled to catch sight of a pale face scowling from the wall. He saw that it was his own face. But he had been startled.

He became even more visibly ill at ease when a voice was raised in some distant room of the house, shouting. The voice came more clearly . . . was approaching. Lachlan Mac Mhuirich fixed his eye on the door.

The Factor gave one look and seeing who it was shouted with laughter. He made a really extraordinary figure just then, standing in the doorway. He had come straight from his bed without troubling to put on his clothes. His black hair was rumpled, standing on end, and his beard in disorder. He wore only his shirt and below it appeared his naked legs which were thick and muscular and of an extraordinary hairiness. But his effrontery was undiminished. Indeed the whole effect of his appearance, his jaunty self-possession in circumstances usually so associated with embarrassment, was one of shocking audacity.

He was laughing. " So it's yersel', Lachlan! The auld wife tell'd me it was a *man* frae Glen Loochry—the doited carlin! " He came into the room and shut the door.

" Sit ye doon, Lachlan, sit ye doon! And tak' aff your bonnet."

At this bantering, contemptuous tone Lachlan Mac Mhuirich adopted a sulky, resentful air. However he looked round and as there was a chair near him he sat down on it, on the edge of the seat, uncomfortably.

The Factor looked at him, and suddenly scowled. "What's

wrang wi' ye that ye canna tak' aff your bonnet? "

The man still hesitated. The Factor's face darkened with sudden rage. He roared, ' Tak' it *aff*, will ye? "

His appearance was terrifying now, Lachlan MacMhuirich took off the bonnet and sat looking up at him with a mixture of apprehension and resentment.

The Factor glared for a moment, then becoming aware of the man's ludicrous appearance laughed again. The top of Lachlan Cearbach's head was unexpectedly quite bald, the Adam's-apple protruded in his scraggy throat, the dead white eye gleaming balefully put, fantastically, two expressions on his face at once—and he presumed to consider his dignity had been hurt!

"Ah weel, Lachlan," said the Factor, relenting, " Ye maun mind your menners."

He sat down in his armchair by the table, in front of Lachlan MacMhuirich, and stuffing the shirt down between his thighs crossed his bare legs and sat with his audacious air, at his ease.

" Weel noo, Lachlan," he said, and he had reverted to his tone of banter, " What is't brings ye? Of course, mind, dinna think we're nae gled tae see yersel' and the freends frae Glen Loochry at ony time. I'm only juist jalousin' that sin' ye come at sic an ungodly 'oor ye'll hae brocht news. Oot wi' it than, Lachlan, an' no haud me sittin' in my sark."

Lachlan MacMhuirich leant towards him, not sulky now but eager all at once.

" Maighstir Sachairi . . . " he said, " Maighstair Sachairi, he . . . "

The Factor sat bolt upright. He clapped his hands down on the arms of the chair. " Oot wi' it, man! "

" Maighstir Sachairi . . . " said Lachlan MacMhuirich, excitedly searching for the words in the foreign tongue, " He wass preach the-day. . . . "

The Factor was leaning forward now as eager as the other. " Oot wi' it, man! What aboot Maister Zachary? Has he come till't? has he come till't? "

Lachlan Cearbach nodded rapidly.

" Yess. He wass come till 't."

The Factor let himself slowly backwards till he was reclining in the chair, his arms along the arms. He smiled, a slow, triumphant smile. With his eyes half-closed, his nostrils expanded, the smile playing on his full lips. he might have been in the act of inhaling some delicious perfume.

But in a moment he sat upright again.

" But are ye sure, man? Ye couldna be mista'en. could ye? "

Lachlan MacMhuirich was looking at him.

" No. I wass hear him myself. All man wass hear him."

The Factor smiled. He was leaning forward towards Lachlan MacMhuirich, his eyes shining.

" Let's hear ye, Lachlan! " he said eagerly. " Gie us the haill way o't. Tak' your time and mak' a guid story."

Lachlan MacMhuirich had his eye fixed on the Factor. He moistened his lips.

" Myself wass aye be saying to Maighstir Sachairi this wass be the shudgment of God. I wass tell him what I wass see myself in Gleann Mór agus an Srath Meadhonach and I wass tell him without doubts, Maighstir Sachairi, the shudgment of God it wass."

"I ken, I ken that," the Factor interrupted. He was scratching his leg in his impatience. " And what said he syne? "

Lachlan MacMhuirich drew his brows together at being interrupted. " On first he wass say . . . Maighstir Sachairi was say . . . Oh no, Lachlan, not God. It wass only the bad Factor."

The Factor, frowning,—" Said he sae! "

" But myself wass say, Oh no, Maighstir Sachairi. you wass be wrong, it wass be the shudgment of God surely. And in Gleann Luachrach too it wass be the shudgment of God. And oh, Maighstir Sachairi, I wass say, it wass be the ill thing to counter the will of God."

"Aye, aye, aye. 'Them that counters Him is aye punished.' I ken. But never mind what I wass say an' you wass say. Come on wi' the story. What happened syne? "

Lachlan MacMhuirich was exhibiting signs of annoyance. He was being interrupted when it was clearly his desire— his way—to tell a tale circumstantially and at length. "Och," he said with a change of manner, " Maighstir Sachairi wass shust come and he wass say, You wass be right all the time, Lachlan; without doubts it wass be the shudgment of God."

He broke off as if that was all and sat looking at the Factor with an offended air.

But the Factor was too intent to notice a small thing such as that he had offended Lachlan MacMhuirich. He had twice already put his hand inside his shirt, displaying his hairy chest, and scratched himself in his impatience. " Weel but what aboot the *story* noo? " he said, urging him. " What did he say? He was preachin', did ye say? Come *on,* man! What ails ye? "

Lachlan MacMhuirich was evidently divided between his sense of having been offended and a desire to tell his tale. Shortly, however, the latter conquered. He fixed his good eye upon the other in a look intended to be portentous and insinuative, leaning slightly towards him with a motion of secrecy, and began again searching and lumbering among his few words of English.

The people of Gleann Luachrach had supposed they would be left alone— this he conveyed. They had gone about their affairs as the season required secure in the thought that Maighstir Sachairi would not let them be molested further. Maighstir Sachairi had even said this, or as much, for he told them to sow, and not to mind the Factor. " But Maighstir Sachairi he wass be gey strange since a week. He wass look . . . " (Lachlan MacMhuirich here distorted his features in an effort to represent Maighstir Sachairi's aspect of unearthly calm; drawing down his mouth and distending his eyes—a fearful grimace, if he had known it. The Factor looked. " Gode be here! " he whispered in pretented alarm, hiding his laughter). Lachlan MacMhuirich related how all Gleann Luachrach had come to the church, fearing the change they detected in Maighstir Sachairi and what it might portend; how the text had spoken of a great and terrible

wilderness and of hunger. . . . He was excited. He related
everything with gestures and movements of his eye, eking
out the quaint combinations and juxtapositions of his few
English words; unconsciously he had fallen into the tone
and manner of a reciter of the traditional tales. When he
came to the point where Maighstir Sachairi sat down he
described his lifeless attitude in the pulpit by sagging forward till his hands trailed limply on the floor and his head
hung down between his knees. Last of all he represented
the people pressing together to get out of the church, by
leaning out to one side and with his face twisted round
looking fearfully back over the other shoulder.

The Factor laughed outright. "Dod! it's like a play! I
hope ye'll no hae hurtit yersel' wi' a' that joukin' aboot."

"H'm," he said, becoming grave again and putting on a
judicial air. "Aye, I doot Zachary will juist hae come till 't.
It looks fell like it."

Lachlan MacMhuirich was watching his face. At this he
leaned forward, till he was nearly out of his chair. He was
trembling with excitement. "*Baile a'mhanaich . . .*" he
whispered in a kind of fevered eagerness.

The Factor looked up, and gave a short barking laugh.
"What!" he cried, with angry contempt, "You? *You* a
fermer? Ye orra shauchle ye, what wad *you* dae wi'
Balivany?"

At this an extraordinary change came over Lachlan
MacMhuirich. His face became dark, his features contorted
with mingled vexation and baffled rage. "You wass promise
. . . you wass promise . . ." he cried in a voice rising out
of control. His hands trembled.

He was trying to lean forward even farther, but was embarrassed by the Factor's toe. The two had been sitting not
far apart, facing. At the first onset of Lachlan MacMhuirich's
excitement the Factor simply stretched out the leg that was
crossed over the other, so that when the man was leaning
farthest forward the naked foot was almost directly below
his chin, and with a gesture of indolent contempt moved
the big toe, in slow jerks, backwards and forwards. Mean-

while he himself lay back in his chair and watched the man carefully, with half-closed eyes.

When he saw the spasm was passing he sat up. "H'm," said he, resuming his judicial air. "H'm, so ye wad like us to gie ye a lease o' Balivany, wad ye? H'm."

He put his head on one side and slowly combed his beard with his fingers, looking at Lachlan mockingly, provocatively, out of the corners of his eyes. "Weel, Balivany is to be vacant shune, richt enough; for Zachary will no get it noo, seein' he keepit us waitin'. But ye wad need to gie us some proof, first of a', that we're in your debt, Maister . . . Maister What-d'they-ca'-ye?"

The man shook his head, he had not understood.

"I'm sayin' hoo are we to ken it was yersel' that brocht him roond?"

"I wass . . . I wass . . . myself wass. . . ."

He struggled to find words. But his excitement was shaking him; he could scarcely articulate. He would have leant forward in his eagerness but the foot was there again; the big toe, which was larger in proportion than usual and stood apart, performing its trick of jerking slowly backwards and forwards. The Factor increased his confusion and excitement by his mocking look, lying back in his chair. He permitted him to stammer and falter into silence. Then he spoke slowly. "It'll maybe surprise ye to ken "— he emphasised each word —'that ye're a leear. Ye had naething a-dae wi' it."

He sat up, holding up his hand. "Haud your wheesht noo! Man ye peetifu' object, d'ye think Maister Zachary wad heed ye?"

He assumed a sly look. "Wad ye like to ken wha brocht Zachary roond?" He pointed to his breast. "Here he is!"

He threw himself back in his chair and indolently re-crossed his legs; and extending his hand with an affectation of gracious condescension said, "Sin' ye've putten versel' to sae muckle trouble I'll mak' a freend o' ye an' tell ye what was the way o't. Juist listen to this.

"Ye maun ken, Lachlan, that at the first Maister Zachary was a sair trial till us and it lookit like he wad coup the haill kettlefu', what wi' the way he wadna hear reason and yon flytin' o' his at Dunechin. But I wasna to be putten oot o' my road, I juist gaed straucht forrit and the neist thing Maister Zachary kent the heather was a-lowe. Weel I lookit to hear something frae him syne, but I had a crack wi' himsel' and what dae ye think?—he never loot dab. Juist sat on his pownie and says, douce-like, Man yon's a peety, yon's a fell peety. Thinks I ye're unco sma'moo'd aboot it the-day; I wonder what's taen ye! So I lookit at him, and damn me if I didna think he didna richtly ken himsel' whether he wanted it to be Yea or Nay.

"When I saw that I cam' awa' hame. For dae ye see Lachlan, if ye want a body that doesna exactly lo'e ye to mak' up his mind the t'ae way, an' he kens that, keep oot o' his sicht or the sicht o' ye 'll gar him mak' it up the t'ither. Ah weel, I cam' hame and I sits doon to think it a' ower. And says I to mysel', Yonder's a man noo that doesna ken his mind. Noo, says I, if ye lay hand on Glen Loochry, Hell mend him but he'll maybe ken it shune eneuch— and I'm a peaceable man d'ye see, Lachlan, I dinna like sodgers and fechtin'. But, says I, juist let him a-be a whilie and it's a wonder gin he'll no come till't o' himsel'. For dae ye ken, Lachlan, there's naething waur nor your mind in twa bits, as ye micht say; gaein' twa roads. 'Aye' and 'No' gaein' roond in your heid. A man canna get his meat taen for thinkin' will it be aye, or will it be no. Afore lang he doesna richtly care which o' them it is if only it wad be ane o' the twa an' be dune wi' 't. And if there's a thing ye're feart o', and it's comin', and aye comin', and never comin'—man dae ye ken efter a while ye wad be gled o' it comin', ye wad even gang half-roads to meet it, only for no tae hae it comin', an' aye comin', and no comin'. Sae I thocht aboot Maister Zachary—he's a man siclike 's oorsels, he'll hear aboot Glen More an' Strath Meeny, thinks I, and if he didna ken his mind afore, that'll bedeevil him fairly. He'll no get sleepin' at nicht for wonderin', What'll I dae? what'll I dae noo? And aye thinkin', It'll be oor turn the morn! But it'll no be, thinks I, for I'll sit at hame like a moosie and Glen

Loochry 'll never see a whisker o' me. And the langer I bide
oot o' sicht and dae naething the mair he'll bedeevil himsel'
wi' wonderin' an' wonderin' and aye thinkin' twa things at
aince; till he'll wish to Gode the warst was dune and owre
wi' and let him get peace. And that'll be my time, thinks I.

"And that's exac'ly hoo it's happened, or I'm mista'en.
Frae what ye're tellin' me I wad say Zachary has gotten
that bedeeviled wi' wonderin' and no kennin' what meenit
to expect the thing he was feart o' that here he's come half
roads to meet it only for no to hae it aye hanging' owre him.

"Juist what I expeckit! Juist what I expeckit!" He smiled
complacently. "Man, I'm a sly ane tae!"

Recollecting himself he at once got briskly to his feet.
"Lachlan, man . . . I'm sorry . . . Ye'll hae till excuse me.
There's things to dae." And he turned to go.

He had taken several steps away from the chair when he
heard a movement behind him. He turned. "Hullo! What's
a' your hurry? Are ye for aff?"

At first when the Factor had silenced him Lachlan Mac
Mhuirich continued for a time to be excited, and to watch
the Factor's face for a sign of an opportunity to speak.
Soon however he seemed to understand that he would not
get an opportunity. The Factor was reclining at his ease,
speaking in his insolent tone of affected candour; his black
eyes were fixed on him with a hint of mockery, but they
were steady, watchful, bullying him and bearing him down,
and seemed to threaten anger at the slightest movement or
provocation. Lachlan MacMhuirich seemed at last to understand the situation, that he had been tricked, and was being
played with. The eagerness and excitement ebbed from him,
and dejection took its place. He sat hanging his head, his
one eye looking up at the Factor, dubiously, and with a kind
of cowed reproach.

When the Factor concluded abruptly and got up to go he
gave a start and rose too, hurriedly. But stopped at once
when the other turned round on him with a threatening
look.

Finding his way barred he stood hesitating, fingering his bonnet nervously. "I wass . . . I wass go home now," he brought out in a voice become high and plaintive.

"Hame?" cried the Factor, raising his brows. "Deil a hame will ye gang oot o' here! It wadna dae ava'. It juist couldna be thocht o'. Ye've brocht Maister Zachary roond. Hoo dae I ken if I let ye gang ye'll no turn him again? Na, na, Lachlan, *I'm* gaein' but *ye're* bidin' whaur ye are." He took a step to go.

But something had been happening to Lachlan during this last speech of the Factor's. From merely glancing about in a nervous, rather frightened manner he had passed all at once—something seemed to strike him—to looking at the Factor, in his face. His eyes widened. A kind of *recognition* dawned in his look. He even drew away a step with a movement of repugnance, staring with horrified fascination at something he appeared to have that minute seen. Just as the Factor turned away he took his head in his hands and broke out in a high, wailing voice, swaying to and fro. "Oh! I wass sinned . . . I wass sinned!"

Unfortunately in the stress of his emotion his few words of the foreign tongue could not suffice him. He broke into Gaelic.

The Factor made a sound in his mouth, an exclamation cut off at the teeth, and was round in the instant. Rage transformed him. His lips were twisted, pressed together, while his brow slowly darkened. His appearance became really terrifying. Even the shirt on him could be seen trembling with his rage.

"Hoo *daur* ye!" he cried when at last he was able to articulate. His voice almost screamed.

Then he got some control of himself. He stamped his bare foot and shouted in a roaring voice. "Ye dog's voamit! Ye . . . ye Hielan' trash! I'll learn ye to speak your dog's gibberish in my hoose!"

Lachlan MacMhuirich had dropped his hands from his head and stood abashed and shaking before the Factor's fury. Perhaps he thought the Factor was about to assault him. He suddenly lost control of himself and on an impulse of flight sprang forward to the door.

The Factor had only to take one step into his path. He shot out both his fists together and caught the man on the chest, something between a blow and a push, and being much the heavier sent him flying backwards. Lachlan MacMhuirich, in falling threw his arms wide. He crashed against the chair he had been sitting on and came down awkwardly on his knees beside it. He knelt there looking up at the Factor. On his upturned face there came an expression, a sort of sweetish look, as of childlike surprise. Suddenly, his face filled with tears.

For his part also the Factor was regarding with a look like amazement the man kneeling on the floor in front of him.

He frowned, and without a word turned and walked to the door, his shirt-tail flapping behind him as he went.

But when he had already reached the door, he stopped. His hand on the latch and his head bowed, he seemed by his air to be considering something. Eventually he asked, over his shoulder—

" Can ye tell me, Lachlan . . . dae ye happen to ken . . . hoo Maister Zachary gaed on the way he did? What was it garred him gang agin us? " His tone was without a trace of his habitual mockery or more recent anger: it was a frank question.

Lachlan MacMhuirich, still kneeling by the chair, gave the Factor a doubtful look. " Maighstir Sachairi wass be a goot man—a *goot* man," he said in a plaintive, tearful voice.

The Factor raised his eyebrows. Looking on the ground he remained a while standing, the fingers of his free hand combing his beard. He put his fist on his hip, still looking down at the floor. At last he shook his head and shrugging his shoulders turned again to go.

But before opening the door he stopped again, turned back. He gave a sharp look at the other. " Here, Lachlan," he said, " I'm thinkin' ye could juist gang hame, efter a'."

He turned as if to open the door, hesitated, and came back once more. " Nae use fashin' the auld wife," he was saying as if speaking to himself, but loud enough for the other to hear. "I'll let ye oot the ither road."

He came up to the table, blew out one candle, and taking up the other walked with it to another door at the side of the room. He had his hand on the latch and looked round over his shoulder. "What is 't, Lachlan? Are ye gaein' or bidin'?"

Lachlan MacMhuirich had got up to his feet the moment the Factor spoke of releasing him. He was standing by his chair looking irresolutely, doubtfully. Thus encouraged he stooped down sideways—but keeping his eye on the Factor —felt with his hand, and picked up his bonnet from where it had fallen when he himself stumbled and fell against the chair. Then he came forward, but with a hesitating step, keeping a little away and looking watchfully, as if he mistrusted this change in the Factor and feared another assault on his person. And with the same look of repugnance and *recognition* in his face.

The Factor did not appear to notice. "Haste ye, Lachlan," he said, encouraging him. "Look, I'll let ye see your road."

He held the door open with one hand while with the other he extended the candle towards Lachlan MacMhuirich, who being in the act of giving him a specially searching glance before venturing to pass in front of him, had his eye momentarily dazzled.

Lachlan made one step past him.

Quick as thought the Factor was behind him and with a violent push sent him headlong into the deep cupboard. In an instant he had closed the door and twice turned the key in the lock.

CHAPTER NINE

A FTER the people had passed out of the church Maighstir Sachairi remained slumped together and motionless in the pulpit seat. After a time a sort of stupor began to supervene over the fearful torment of his thoughts. Once or twice he raised his head and looked about him dully. But by this time he understood nothing, not even perceiving where he was.

Then a very strange thing happened. He fell suddenly fast asleep. For a single moment he seemed as if resisting, tried to sit upright. Then sleep rushed on him. In an instant he was so deeply sunk in it that nothing would have roused him. And gradually, as he slept, the stern features softened and relaxed, the look of suffering passed away. By and by a faint, wonderfully blissful smile appeared flitting over his face.

The hours passed. It was so quiet in the church that the occasional buzz of a fly broke loudly on the stillness: and when it settled the gentle, regular breathing of the sleeper began once more to be clearly heard.

Evening drew on and still he slept, his head pillowed on his hand. At length shadows began to fill the church. The darkness slowly deepened. Stars appeared. All night across the windows their array swung slowly down. But the figure in the pulpit never stirred.

Not even when there rose up all around the church a deafening clamour of birds singing in the hour before the dawn. . . .

2

The day broke clear, with patches of mist soon dispelled before a light breeze blowing from the west.

In Gleann Luachrach smoke still hung thinly above many of the roofs, as though the people had been but lately around the hearths. And shortly the fires were replenished, for the smoke began to pour out thickly from chimneys and roof-tops where it hung above the houses in widening clouds before drifting away eastwards.

The family in the miller's house were among the first to be afoot. None of its adult members had slept during the night. Since they had returned home the previous day not a word had been spoken about the scene in the church nor reference of any kind made to it. But through the silent afternoon and evening, and later when, the children being abed, they sat about the hearth without speaking till far into the night, each knew that that, and the fear of what it portended, were the sole subject of the others' thoughts. At another time a common trouble or perplexity would have sent them to their knees together, but that in this case would have been to make admission of their fears and so to give them reality in the mind. But in the night the miller, who may have begun to doze, felt his wife move beside him and opened his eyes hearing a low exclamation from her. Although she did not move again he knew that she was lying awake, and somehow he knew that she was listening. Then he heard it himself—the voice grumbling and muttering, sometimes breaking off suddenly and becoming inaudible, at others rising until the words could almost be distinguished, then again falling to a grumble and a murmuring. He recognised Gilleasbuig Liath's voice. He must have been praying in his bed: he was getting so deaf of late that he had no control over the volume of his voice, did not know how loudly he was speaking. As the miller listened to those tones of pleading, of supplication in the night, the forebodings took hold afresh upon his mind.

Almost before the light they were up and moving. Gilleasbuig Liath knew it and began knocking loudly on the wall of his room with his stick. The miller went to him and helping him out of bed began to dress him as usual: then taking his arm helped him through to the living room of the house where Peigi Dhonn was kindling up the fire, and settled him in his chair. All the while not a word passed between them: indeed they openly avoided looking at each other, averting their eyes.

The same silence and constraint brooded over the meal. Only the appetites of the younger children seemed little affected by it. Their fears were no more than the vague reflection of what was sensed as a parental mood, and could not survive the out of doors, the light of day, the onset of the impulse to play in company of their fellows, and all the bright real things of the world which in the fresh perceptions of childhood tend to joy. Very soon their laughter could be heard as they romped outside the house. The miller too got up and went out as soon as he had finished toying with his meal, and the lad Eachann with him. Peigi Dhonn immediately set about her morning's work.

Her house had always been a great care to her, to keep it spotless in every nook and corner. Yet to-day it was as if she had suddenly become *conscious* of her house, of doors and walls and windows, of every chair and table as she went about, of every dish even, their shapes and colours, the very marks and scratches they had acquired in the years (she kept recalling the occasions), so that probably she had never been so thorough. At the same time she felt strangely withdrawn into herself, working about in silence. She could not have explained it, but to-day she touched everything, lingered over it, almost with affection, and in some curious way was both happy and sorrowful doing it.

Once in passing the window she paused and looked out. That scene was as familiar to her as her house itself. For twenty years there had not been a day when she had not looked out on that same portion of the glen, and seen it in all the changes of the turning seasons, sunbathed as now, with a movement of cloud shadows, or large though mist, or again rain-lashed, or white under snow, so that it was as familiar, every feature and contour of it, almost as her own body—and again there came over her that strange feeling that was like wonder or a kind of *consciousness*, as if

she had never really seen it until now. The curve of the
stream in the glen bottom, tree bordered at intervals, the
houses on the right-hand slopes; high up on the left the
manse, and a portion of the white walled church behind it,
just above the track leading down from the upper portion
of the glen: all seemed to have become curiously new, or
real—as if what she had hitherto been familiar with had
only been a picture, and this was the living scene. Bright and
smiling it all looked this morning and Peigi lingered. Under
the influence of its solid aspect of realness and familiarity the
numb anxiety of her mind was for the moment soothed
away.

She was in the act of turning from the window when some
thing or movement in the scene caught her attention. She
turned back and looked again. At first she could not pick
it out, whatever it had been. But she found her eyes searching the line of the low ridge that ended the view of the right
hand slope of the glen. If it had been something there, there
was nothing to be seen now. But—yes, even as her eyes
travelled back along the ridge a part of it seemed to quiver.
She looked more closely and saw that a faint blur or darkness had appeared as it were hanging above it. It was very
faint and in a moment was no longer there. Then it reappeared, darker this time. Smoke. There were two houses
with their steadings just there, out of sight beyond the ridge,
and sometimes on calm days the smoke from their chimneys
could be seen in thin spirals. But to-day the landscape had
a look of wind; and this was a cloud of smoke—a thick
cloud now. A look of concern crossed her face as the thought
occurred to her, watching, that something must be on fire
yonder.

Strangely enough it was not till a moment later that a
terrible suspicion crossed her mind. She cried out, her face
going white, then glanced nervously over her shoulder at
Gilleasbuig Liath. But the old man had not heard and was
sitting withdrawn as he had been all the morning, glooming
into the fire. In the instant it took her to see this the smoke
cloud above the ridge had become much denser. Yet below

the ridge it must have been denser still for the wind was blowing it away to eastward. She watched it in a sort of fascination, the colour draining slowly from her face.

Quite suddenly an irregular knot of men had appeared on the slope, advancing down it towards a house that stood near the river, below the ford. There was a spot of fire in their midst. When she saw that her lips went white. " Oh. Dhia, Dhia, teine, teine! "—" Oh, God, God, fire, fire! " she exclaimed in a little voice like a moan. It was certain now. She stood blenched, rigid, following the rapid advance of the group on the slope, unable to take her eyes from them. They had almost reached the foot before she came to herself with a kind of start, and at once leaned forward, straining her eyes to the left, where the mill could just be seen.

But the miller was already close at hand, coming towards the house, the lad Eachann at his back. One look at him coming in and she knew that he had seen it too. He came over and stood beside her, and both looked away again down the glen. Not a word passed between them. The lad had remained outside, by the door.

They saw the group of figures reach the house and pass out of sight. Then Peigi Dhonn found a voice—" The old woman, Tormod! Run! " The miller glanced once towards Gilleasbuig Liath, saw that he was still too sunken and absorbed to have noticed anything as yet, and went out. Peigi Dhonn at the window first saw Eachann spring into sight and go off down the glen, running hard. Then the miller's broad form came into view. Every now and then he broke into a heavy run for a few steps, then hurried forward as fast as he was able, working his arms.

She saw Eachann reach the house and disappear. As she watched figures appeared at the gable, disappeared, appeared again. She found herself wondering in numb fashion what they were about, so busily.

By this time the miller had still covered little more than half the ground. Her eyes measured the distance between the house by the river and the bulky figure labouring resolutely towards it. Above, the smoke was hanging in an even heavier cloud along the ridge. She found herself wondering with a sudden strange impersonality—for all at once the realisation that the matter affected *her* had slipped from the grasp of her mind—whether the hurrying figure could reach the house before a similar cloud began to rise above it also.

Now he had almost reached it. . . .

Something made her turn her eyes to the right. A shudder passed over her. Her jaw dropped with a kind of stricken helplessness, while her eyes slowly distended, until they seemed to stir from their sockets. Another party had been descending the slope behind the miller's house, and so were already almost upon it before they came into view from the window.

Gilleasbuig Liath heard her shriek and was looking round at her. All at once he began trying helplessly to rise out of his chair, shaking violently all over.

3

When Maighstir Sachairi awoke at last he passed without the normal slow dawning of the senses and the mind straight into full awareness and activity. One instant he was sunk in a still and immobile slumber in which for hours there had appeared no lightening; the next he was up and thundering down the pulpit steps.

The empty shell of the building as he strode through it was full of dark moving shadows and lights that flashed and flickered redly, its hollow depths and recesses vocal with strange half-cries and muted shouting. He flung wide the door and stood upon the threshold. The suddenly no longer moderated lights and noises crashed upon his senses and for the instant stunned him. But with a cry he stepped forward, stepped this way then that as if confused; then turned and bounded round the end of the building. Once as he ran he shouted " *Lachlan!* " but did not stay his running.

In the stable the sounds were muted again; the horse was moving restlessly, stamping in its stall. Without hesitating he went to its head, and slipping on the bridle calmed it with words.

Once outside words would no longer calm it; it plunged and snorted, thrashing out with its legs. The minister held it firmly by mane and bridle and when it would have galloped off pulled it round by the head and in a moment leaped upon its back. Several times it wheeled wildly round in circles in its tracks, trying to unseat him, but he held it with his knees and was its master. A shifting of the wind had turned the smoke and of a sudden there fell around them a choking dusk, through which only the white wall of the church was a dim glimmer. The wind shifted again, the smoke and the loud clamour fled away backward, the wall gleamed out whitely then turned a steady red. Maighstir Sachairi turned the plunging beast remorselessly and striking with his heels drove it down the slope.

There was no hesitation in him now. That nearly thirty hours' oblivion had washed away to the last hesitation the disorder and strained perplexity of his mind: when he woke there was no problem before him, the world had righted itself in his perception. Now again, his horizons no longer conscience-clouded, things were themselves. The horse slipped sideways, recovered, slid forward almost on its haunches, ploughing the stones and earth before its outspread feet. He held it to its wild descent and kept his seat as by a miracle. Coming to lower ground he freed the reins and driving in his heels thundered across the level.

But reaching the river bank he reined in violently and turned aside, peering beyond him. There was a movement in the ford. In a moment a man came up out of the river carrying an old man on his back. Three others followed carrying something in a plaid between them; climbing the bank they swayed and staggered under its weight. Then one with a bundle in his arms. In the dusk cast by the heavy pall that overcast the sky they passed him without a look or a word spoken and turned down the glen. Hot gusts were coming down the wind. In the river bed the sounds came more clearly and distinctly though diminished in volume.

From following with his eye the retreating group of figures he chanced to glance behind: the whole slope he had descended was stained a bright blood colour, with dark ripplings like cloud shadows moving across it in ceaseless rapid undulation. He turned and at once entered the stony ford.

At its farther end had been the house of Eoghann Ogha-Duibhne. The breath of the wind passed over the red shell that remained of it and little flames came out in the walls and on the glowing heap made by the burnt-out interior and fallen roof. He had already seen that in the whole eastward or lower part of the glen the flames had even now done their work and were already dying away, therefore he did not pause but bore away to the right and upwards, in the path of the fire-makers.

As he rode the wind ever and anon freshening in long gusts brought down the smoke in billows pouring towards him above the ground, and then horse and man were coughing and choking: and dying again let the grey acrid blanket thin slowly away, to reveal the red glares of a score or over of homes and their outbuildings before and on the slope above him in flames at once, each sending up one of the long living pillars to support the moving red-shot pall that roofed the whole glen over. In those intervals they were able to make forward rapidly over familiar ground, the horse however answering ever more nervously to its urging on, breaking into short gallops, checking, trying to wheel about, then, urged again, sliding away sideways under the rider, rolling a fright-haunted eye. From time to time on the ground about them there was a scurrying of the small fry of animals making their escape.

But the wind grew ever steadier, less intermittent. With the smoky blanket down came the heat. The sounds began to be clearer: it was no longer always the one dominant noise, continuous but confused and fluctuating; more and more individual voices could be heard within its mass, voices that started up and running their course ended abruptly or faded back into the general clamour. Clearest were women's voices, then children's. There were voices of fear, of supplication, of pain, and anger, of lamentation, and the brutal voice of exulting laughter. Each stung the rider to a yet more eager and impetuous progress in spite of the obscurity. He rode hunched forward in the saddle, his eyes, bloodshot and smarting from the smoke, peering about on the ground to make the track.

That way they once came near disaster. Almost before they became aware of a glow lighting up the smoky gloom ahead, they were out upon an unroofed building standing in their path, the flames still leaping high inside. Even as they quickly turned aside from it the near gable bent and fell outward with a dismal crash. The horse leapt and quivered as the sparks shot in a fiery cataract round its very feet: Maighstir Sachairi made use of its excitement to let it out in a blind gallop straight ahead.

Therewith confusion quickly grew. On all sides now were the shrieks of women, the roar and crackle of flames, men shouting, the crash of falling roofs and buildings, dogs barking, howling, yelping, the bellowing of terrified cattle charging through the smoke. Hell and Babel. Now shapes were everywhere: moving dimly nearby in the surging grey, or, in a lifting, appearing black against some conflagration on the slope. The heat at times was murderous. All about them there was a sort of rain of glowing particles. And the stench of burning wood and peat and thatch compounded had become insufferable. The horse had at length perceived that its headlong course was taking it towards the source of more affright and began refusing to go forward, jerking violently this way and that, trampling the spot, and more than once wheeling several times in circles before its head could be brought to it again. It was incessantly stretching out its neck and giving vent to a hoarse coughing—as did its rider between the shouts with which he urged it on.

Quite suddenly they came upon a section of the burning party at work. A house had just been set well on fire and smoke was rising through the roof and pouring in thick masses out of the windows and the open door. Occasionally there was a flash of flame. Some of the people of the house were standing a little apart beside a heap of their belongings that they had been able to drag away in time to safety. But Maighstir Sachairi's eyes were all for the others, on whom one by one he directed a stern, attentive scrutiny. For it was not easy at a glance to recognise any under the wild appearance they presented, their hands and faces covered over with soot and ashes of the burning houses cemented by grease and sweat.

Even at a glance however their half-drunken condition was apparent.

There were five of them. They were spread out in a half-circle before the house. Every now and then one or other amid drunken yells would dash away after one of the domestic animals trying to escape, and having caught it would throw it back into the flames; while the shouts and laughter redoubled.

So intent were they that it was some time before they became aware of the figure on the dancing horse observing them. Then first one, then the others in turn stiffened and became motionless in the attitude in which awareness found them, while the laughter died thinly. Even the drink cooled in them visibly as the eyes of each became fixed with an instant apprehension on him who sat there.

The first fright passed. Then a movement of uneasiness went over them. Glances were cast to right and left. It seemed that in another moment the whole party must have broken into precipitate flight.

But at that moment Maighstir Sachairi, having finished passing from one to the other with his slow regard and not having found him among them whom he sought, calmly withdrew his eyes and fixed them on another small party of two or three a little beyond, who were not yet aware of him and whose drunken shouts meantime continued to offend the air. The house was built not far from a pretty steep precipice that overhung the river, and these were gathered on the edge of it. Nearby they had collected a number of the wooden chests in which the people were accustomed to preserve their meal. One after the other they carried between them to the brink and dispatched down the precipice with shrieks and yells, their sport being to see the boxes broken to atoms and the meal mixed with the air. Maighstir Sachairi applied to them the same stern scrutiny, his eyes passing unhurried over each in turn. Meanwhile those below were still held in their uneasiness, clearly disposed towards flight but at the same time fearful of what their first movement might bring down upon them. From the house, now well alight, came a series of crackling reports as loud as pistol shots. Maighstir Sachairi finished his scrutiny at his own time and without wasting another look turned about.

And in the act of turning saw him—at last! Coming towards him. Out of the smoke, like a fiend from the Pit. At sight of him Maighstir Sachairi stiffened, then without taking his eyes from him edged his horse forward so that he would be bound to meet him face to face. Being not far from the farthest point the burning parties had reached as yet, and the wind blowing fresh, the space between them was clear of smoke and he was plainly to be seen. As he came on he staggered drunkenly, looking on the ground. He was so grimed and spattered with soot and ash that he might have suggested some creature whose home and element was fire. Maighstir Sachairi's head was thrust forward and his glance never left him; his frown was partly questioning, as if he were trying to decide in his mind what state the man was in. As he came nearer it could be seen that he was pale under the grime that streaked his face, no longer ruddy. He had not apparently recognised the minister or even noticed his approach, and seeing this Maighstir Sachairi drew up his horse after a time and waited, still studying him.

He had almost collided with the horse before he was aware of it standing in his path. Then he stood still, and slowly raised his eyes till he was looking up under his brows at the rider. His eyes had the glazed uncertain look of drunkenness—what made this terrible in him was that this drunkenness was not from drink, in which the man was never overtaken. Although he was looking up with a dazed

intentness into his face he did not at once recognise Maighstir
Sachairi. When he did a look of triumph passed over his
relaxed features. A slow malicious smile came and played
about his mouth. He raised his arm in a stiff gesture above
his head: the stiffness of it carrying his garments up about
his ears behind so that he was for the moment as if hump-
backed or deformed.

"They're doon noo, Maister Wiseman!" he cried in a
high excited voice, not his own, a point of mad excitement
dancing in his eye. "They're doon noo!" He closed his fist
and shook it in drunken emphasis—"Ye'll—*never*—big
them again!"

"Call off your men, Factor!" the minister was shouting,
distracted by difficulty in controlling his horse which had
been startled afresh by the Factor's voice and gesture and
had slid away, leaping and plunging. "Call off your men!"
he shouted, bringing it up again.

"Never!" the factor roared, right at the horse's face—
"Never, Maister Wiseman!—I *hae* them!"

What Maighstir Sachairi would have replied will never be
known. At that instant came a sudden and violent interruption. From away on the left, where the smoke hung thickly,
arose a sound like thundering hoofs, coming nearer. Both
turned to look, not without apprehension. The noise
approached rapidly. Horns appeared tossing in the smoke.

It all happened in an instant. The horse shuddered under
him, scenting the danger, then reared up in air. By instinct
to avoid the pawing hoofs the Factor sprang aside, staring upwards. (What he saw in that momentary glance he was to
remember once more, and once again when his hour came:
Maighstir Sachairi's snow-white hair blowing, the look of
doom he bent on him, the forefinger he raised above his
head, seeming to appeal straight upward through the smoke-
filled sky). Then the cattle were on them. The Factor was
struck by one beast's shoulder and went down—fortunately
the animal was on the outside of the group and threw him
clear, or he would have ended there. For the minister it
went less well. The horse had already been brought to the

highest point of nervousness; when the cattle appeared rushing towards them it became quite unmanageable, reared and plunged again, then just as it seemed the charging beasts must have engulfed them darted away in wild career. Maighstir Sachairi saw the course it took and perceiving at once what must happen strove with all his might, desperately, to get it under some control. But the animal had its head and, mad with fear, could neither be brought to moderate its headlong course nor turned aside from it.

At length it saw the danger: but too late; they were already above the precipice. One frantic effort it made to arrest its course, but its pace had been too great; it was carried forward driving stones and earth before it across the brink. A shout from Maighstir Sachairi, drowned at once in a fearful long-drawn scream from the frenzied beast, and they went headlong over to the rocks beneath.

It was a moment or two later before the Factor got to his feet. He had been partly stunned by the violence of his fall, though otherwise unhurt. He looked all about him, seeming surprised to find no one in sight. Then, either not sufficiently sobered to wonder at the minister's disappearance, or careless of it, looked down at himself, ran his hands over his body feeling for hurts, and finally picked up his bonnet from the ground and continued on his way.

CHAPTER TEN

SLOWLY—the movement gave him infinite pain—Maighstir Sachairi raised his eyelids. For a space he remained quite still, trying to come to himself. When slowly and gradually the external resumed its inward flow, bringing consciousness, he recognised first of all the object that was lying under his eyes. It was a plaid. He considered it a long while, his eyes with pain moving over its uneven surface. It extended away from him, and he could discern the shape of a recumbent form under it, which he saw on slow reflection could only be his own body. He perceived that he was lying on a couch, a plaid laid over him. Even so simple a fact cost him effort to take it in. When he had done so, and felt that he was able to support a further consciousness, he raised his eyes yet a little and looked for a time into the region—dim at first—beyond his feet. Dim shapes there began to define themselves before his gaze—and the forms they took were familiar. There was a chair: an irregular dark shape was a row of books along the wall. This familiarity troubled Maighstir Sachairi a long time.

Then at last he understood, and he was so weak now that the simple act of recognition was almost more than he could bear; he felt he would sink swooning again, and the sweat broke out on his face. It was his own room. He was lying in his study, on his couch, lying covered with a plaid. He now perceived that it must be night, for there was a lamp burning in the room; somewhat behind him, to the left, not far away. There was a deathlike quiet.

All at once it was broken by a sound, a little sound, clear in the stillness, as if someone near him had drawn a long breath like a sigh. Slowly, because of his weakness and the excruciating pain it caused him, he turned his head.

A figure was sitting on a chair by his couch. Quite still: the head bent forward and the chin on the breast. The face —the lamplight fell full on it—was blackened as if by smoke, the hair singed. An open wound, now healing, ran from the brow upwards across the scalp under the hair. The blood had run down and lay thick and darkly congealed on one cheek and clotted among his beard.

At first Maighstir Sachairi supposed that he must be seeing a figure out of his delirium: it was certainly no more real— less real-seeming indeed—than the crowd of figures, some strange-familiar, some merely wild phantasmal creatures of a brain in fever, that had moved becking and grimacing through the endless night of his affrighted dreams. But there was one circumstance; this one's breast—he could see it— moved faintly with his breathing. With that something like a faint memory came back to him: he seemed to remember coming to himself once already, long before—it was night then too, the lamp was lit—and that a voice spoke to him, before he sank again in torment and raving. And there had been other times too, it seemed to him now, during the long long while of his submersion in a sea of pain, when he *was* pain, and consciousness had no content but his suffering; times when he had been aware though dimly of hands holding him, ministering to him, and of a soothing voice.

He regarded the figure closely—the smallish old man, his breast moving gently as he breathed quietly and evenly as if in sleep.

He now thought to address him. But he found himself too weak to speak. He could only, with difficulty, move his lips. Several times he moved them, forming words. He tried to call up all his powers—and at length his tongue moved and an inarticulate sound came from his mouth.

The figure stirred. "You have come to, Maighstir Sachairi. Thank God!" The quiet, matter-of-fact tone somehow conveyed the impression he had been aware of Maighstir

Sachairi's return to consciousness, and waiting for him to speak.

Maighstir Sachairi now knew that he was real and no hallucination. He felt his strength slowly returning to him, though in small, very small measure. Soon, he felt, he would be able to speak the question that was burning in his mind.

The answer came without his asking. "They are on the shore at Camus Bàn," said the old man, unmoving still. "They are without shelter of any kind as yet—and for food they eat shellfish."

He appeared to sink again into his sleep or brooding. Though the quiet tone was the same there had seemed at the last phrase to be some hesitation, some emotion.

Maighstir Sachairi lay quiet.

The figure spoke again—in the same tone, again answering the question that had come into Maighstir Sachairi's mind: so that he wondered for a moment whether he could have spoken it without knowing.

"I myself brought you on my back, Maighstir Sachairi; there was nowhere else. You were lying among the rocks below Poll a'Bhodaich." He added: "I thought at first you must have been dead."

Maighstir Sachairi was farther than ever from speaking now. The dreadful pain had returned and was devouring him. His chest seemed encircled by a band of molten steel, the deepening agony in his staring eyes measured its slow contraction. Then came the moment when suffering reached its apex. The eyelids dropped quivering, the lips were drawn back from the teeth, while the agonising spasm passed through the tortured body.

It passed again; the torturing flood flowed back a little way. The features relaxed. Sweat broke in rivers on his face and brow.

He was weaker now. His eyes rested with a kind of helpless eloquence on the man who sat never changing his position on the chair beside him; as if he would have said much to him if he had been able. Yet in his expression there was nothing of striving or impatience, only kindness, kindness and an unearthly far serenity. All at once he felt himself speaking—quite clearly, though halting, and his voice but a rustling.

"*It was pride, Fearchar, I understand now. I saw myself . . . in the centre . . . too much . . . in the centre . . . That is always pride . . . So great a fault . . .*" and after a pause to gather his resources, "*God knows . . . what use I have been . . .*" From Fearchar came again the long expiration like a sigh. "You did what you saw right, Maighstir Sachairi." Although the sadness of a world was in his tone, there was no hint either of reproach or repining. Fearchar too was passed through the dark night of sorrow to a purging acceptance.

Maighstir Sachairi was speaking again, with difficulty, in a voice yet more nearly inaudible:

"At Camus Bàn, Fearchar—did you say—*all?*"

Fearchar's head drooped lower on his breast.

"Not all, Maighstir Sachairi."—He spoke not without effort, with pauses and hesitations; yet his tone still came quiet as through contemplation of the things he spoke of—"Bean na h-Airde Móire is dead. Even as they carried her out: her very clothes in flames. Some old man is wandering among the rocks at Carnan. I don't know who: he ran from me—barking like a dog."—Here he stopped altogether for a little—"Mairi-of-Eoghann-Gasda fell from the roof of the house and lay in labour before all that stood by: and the child was born before its time and had no life in it. . . ."

But Maighstir Sachairi did not hear him. This time he was spared the agonising onset and had sunk again in merciful oblivion.

*   *   *   *

. . . *the sea was green about the iron coast. The granite cliffs and shattered rocks grey, yellow-flecked, and grey again beneath an inconstant sun flashing through flying clouds. The snoring wind smelt of the sea, salty and fresh, a faint but heady something in it like a fragrance that it might have captured in its thunderous passage through the forest pines of Norway. All along resounding miles the ocean boomed and stilled, boomed and stilled again, like a pulse, and the spray in a cloudy mist went flying inland over the coast and the grey city standing by the sea.*

But One was lacking who had been there that day. From where he sat on a rock in a hollow facing the wind he searched the shore for his familiar form. And laughed again when he saw him standing there and gesturing:—just as it had been then—where the sea rushed through a deep and narrow cleft into the land he was standing astride, and with stick raised, and bending towards the striving tide below, beat out its surging measure on the air. He laughed to see him so absorbed, and because of something dear and living in the man, so typically wrapt away in the unboundedness of elemental things. The sea slipping and surging in below his straddling feet charged up the rocky cleft, and meeting before its strength was spent, with a resounding slap, the perpendicular wall that ended it, was sent skywards in a tower of flashing spray behind which for the time of its descent the gesturing figure disappeared.

He sat at ease, idly remarking how the leaping tower once flashed silver, then, in the sun, twice golden. The long hush, the o'ercome of retiring waves, was already rising all along the coast before the sharp slap came and the glittering fountain spouted, never quite in the expected place, among the rocks. After the heavy splashing of the backward-falling spray, a pause, a moment's silence, a whisper mounting with awful swiftness to a grinding and a tremulant roar, and then the mile-loud boom.

At first he could not understand what had suddenly happened to the scene before him. The green sea still moved rhythmically, forwards and back, and whitened at its verge; the sun glided and ran and glittered over the rocks and the sea; the tall form reappeared gesturing each time the silvery sometimes golden fountain tumbled; there was ever the fine spray blown inland in a misty cloud over the coastward fields. Yet with some difference.—And then he realised that the whole scene had fallen silent: sound had suddenly been subtracted from it; and what he now saw was but a picture of coloured shapes in motion. Oddly, the realisation occa-

sioned him no surprise; he continued with quiet enjoyment to regard the scene before him, in which indeed the effect of motion seemed heightened by the change, outlines made clearer, colours intensified. He felt the spray blown cold over his face, and his hair and beard drenched with it.

So wet indeed that he drew his hands over his eyes and down his face to clear away the streaming water.

With that he was coming up out of the river. He wrung the water out of his hair, slapped and rubbed himself all over vigorously, (scarcely finding it strange that he could not feel his hands touch his body, though he quite clearly felt the moisture running on him), and sat down upon the bank. What a brilliant day that was! Not a cloud; the sky a flawless dome, so delicate; the fresh-clad world rejoicing in the sun.

Abruptly, sound returned. All at once the trees rustled as well as moved their leaves and branches in a lazy movement of the air; the river sang as well as sparkled in the shallows, with a sibilant ripple and a tinkle now and then where the smooth surface of deeper water broke round a large boulder lying in the river bed.

He must have dozed, sitting in the sunshine on the grassy bank, for he seemed to come to himself when he heard the loud hiss of the water breaking round the boulder, and farther up, the river shouting in the shallows. He looked round in sudden alarm, and his heart contracted when he saw the naked figure reclining on the flat top of the boulder, his face turned towards the water as if brooding or dreaming indolently over it in the sun, oblivious of the treachery that threatened him. He shouted. The other raised his head, and in that instant both saw the spate with amazement and fully perceived his danger; and without a moment's delay or hesitation sprang up, poised a second on the boulder, and had launched himself towards the bank.

Even with his powerful strokes he was carried far before he came to it. He grinned, grasping the hand held out to him. Standing on the bank, he was panting, but he soon gave a gay and careless laugh—" Thank ye, Zachary! What did I tell ye—the sea or the river, I'll droon yet!" He looked at the tall

*figure, smiling, debonair, and thought, his heart still con-
tracted: " YOU have not just seen your dearest, your one
friend, in death's very mouth!"—but entering into his mood,
said with a mock-mournful grin, " If ye do, Jonathan, the
Kirk'll tine a silly member—and I'll never forgie ye. Mind
I've tell't ye!"*

Their laughter rose gustily.

*The game at its height, their faces red and strenuous.
The turnip rolled this way and that over the road, and they
leapt after it, smiting with their sticks. " I have ye, Zachary!"
cried the other, sending the turnip rolling. " No' yet!" cried
Zachary leaping back, striking with all his might. There was
a loud crack, the turnip continued rolling. He was looking
down where the stick was broken off just below his hands. A
peal of laughter ringing in his ears.*

*There was a flash in which they were walking along a broad
road by the river. It was winter; ice was floating down in
masses on the water. Their conversation—sombre that day—
echoed frostily.*

*Then all at once he was sitting alone in his lodging, by the
table, at the window. He knew himself again, so strangely
(like another person), in that thirty-years-departed and forgotten mind and consciousness—those headless inspirations,
urgent, unfixed expectancies, wide to the new scarce-glimpsed
dimensions of manhood and the world.*

*Familiar footsteps sounded: someone had come in, closed
the door, put his back against it. Jonathan. Debonair; smiling
his mocking smile. Pointing an accusing finger—" Zachary!
' ABEST ' again, or I'm mista'en!" His glance travels to the
table—" So then! I believe it's the poetry that keepit ye! A
fine state o' affairs this! Ceevil war amang the Humanities!
Poetry agin the Arts!" He threw his books aside with a careless gesture. " What's your theme, Zachary?"*

*Zachary shrugged, ignoring the question—"Weel, Jonathan,
hoo's a' at the Collège the-day?"*

The other struck an attitude and began declaiming—

> " *Auld Grumlie wags his roosty pow,*
> *Wi' meikle smeddum dings doon Cain.*
> *And aye he skelps his buik, and syne*
> *The stoor flees up in cloods again.* "

(*singing*)

> " *Oh, I canna thole 't, I canna thole 't,*
> *And gin I could I wouldna!*
> *Sic orra sneeshin steeked my neb,*
> *And langer bide I couldna!* "

They both burst out laughing.

But immediately that passed away, and now they were sitting again in the accustomed places, over against each other, at either side of the hearth. No word was passing, but the multitudinous echoes of endless conversations and still longer silences stood solidly about them.

The silence lengthened. Now something oppressive and premonitory began to be charged upon it. He looked across at Jonathan—and saw with a remembered pang that he was slowly fading from his sight. First the head—the face was already indistinct: he strained in vain to catch once more those familiar and to him incomparable features; before his very eyes they faded away. Now the whole head was merged and enveloped in the mist or greyness that was spreading down remorselessly. He felt a chill like death begin creeping round his heart, and turned his eyes away. When he brought himself to look again nothing of the figure sitting there was solid but its legs, only the long legs still crossed in a careless manner that he knew well. Then only the feet remained, and above them in the chair a grey indistinctness, and the feeling of a breathing presence thinning slowly away . . . When he looked again the chair was empty, and the room was empty, even of its echoes, and his own heart in his chilly breast was crusted and hollow, like a rotten nut.

He heard their feet outside the door. When they came in, too, it was only their feet he saw. Then he was aware of his own feet following theirs. He knew it was a bright sun that day, but to him its light was only blackness, and of the throng

*about him in the streets he was aware of none, not even as
shadows among shadows—only the feet, his and theirs, like
the rearguard of doom, passing onwards.*

*They had stopped. Now they were talking to him—telling
him how it had befallen: but he heard only an empty sound
of voices. At one sight of that shrouded form the horizon,
which the friendship of One had made boundless, rushed inward to his very feet. And all that he saw was a pool that
slowly gathered there, and gathered, and began to run along
the ground. Looking at it he heard again the sombre echoes
of his footsteps in the street, and knew that they had been his
own life, the old life, the life of his young youth, going backwards and away from him, forever. One man had been that
youth, that life; he lay here; his setting was the night of light-
someness. He had loved him more than his own soul, sinfully
it seemed, not without idolatry; and how terribly the sin was
punished: friendship might live henceforward, but no more
the Friend—forever.*

*That scene, too, swam mistily away. One glimpse he had of
that later scene—God's hand accepted, the window opened
and his trash of rhymes, the fruit of folly and vain years,
blown by the wind among the roofs: then by a gesture that
was final the window closed alike on youth and blithesome-
ness, and his turning away to Duty . . .*

But that ancient pain had been reawakened in full measure,
and such was the agony that as if to escape it he fled upwards
to consciousness and the lesser, bodily torment.

*   *   *   *

When he opened his eyes the light of day was in the room.
Fearchar had not moved from his place. He had raised his
head and the light from the window which faced him fell full
on his blood-stained face. He was looking straight before him
into the light, but as in a dream, unseeingly. From his eyes
the tears flowed down continuously in a quiet stream.

Maighstir Sachairi looked at Fearchar, but was too weak to
speak to him. He might have said a word had he had strength,
but it was too late now; he had no time. The pain had ab-

ruptly left him, but so had feeling: he could no longer see
the walls: Fearchar had grown indistinct: the world was
fading . . .

*   *   *   *

*The Sabbath dusk lay in the room. The ticking of the clock
that swung by the wall, measured, globular, doled out the
Sabbath quiet. Where a shaft of light came through the close-
drawn curtains his father sat again, poring, with many groans
and sighs, upon the Book. Grown tired, no one attending, he
gradually slipped down from the chair he was perched on till
he felt the solid floor under his boots . . .*

*Now he was standing in the passage between the two ends
of the house. There was a narrow wedge of light cutting the
darkness; and he became excited to see the outer door ajar.
He tiptoed up, only to give one look outside.*

*It is bright outside. His dog is there, scratching by the
stable wall. He says its name softly, but it does not hear, and
after shaking itself briskly trots off with a dejected air round
the corner of the wall . . .*

*How long he had been running and gambolling with the
dog about the braes he could not tell; but it seemed long,
when what he was doing suddenly came upon him. He became afraid, with the fear not of earthly things, but of one
seeing Eye: and immediately was running all the way home
with the breath in his breast . . .*

*Somehow it increased his fear wonderfully to find every-
thing exactly as it had been, in the house. When he had stood
a little while in the room and nothing took place, no sudden
awful thing, he became even more afraid. He went and stood
right in front of his father, where he was BOUND to notice
him. His father gave him no more than a half-glance, half-
said his name, abstractedly, and went on reading . . .*

*He was sitting, white-faced, with his food before him. They
asked him why he did not eat, and he was silent . . .*

*Now it was the moment he had dreaded:—in the dark,
alone with his sin—and that Eye! He lay trembling. If only—
he felt—if only his father had punished him: he would have
felt so sad and safe, so sorry and secure. How was it possible*

his father would not know when a little boy had been break-ing the Sabbath, playing on the Sabbath day? When he thought of that—that his father had not KNOWN, was not all-knowing—the earth seemed dissolving under him, and the ambient dark stirred full of menace.

He must have slept, for he woke shrieking in the night; and lay not daring to breathe, while the echoes of his shriek-ing died away. Into silence. He had never heard such silence. As if he were all alone—alone— He could not control his sweat and quaking when the thought came: Christ had come; while he was sleeping Christ had come into the air and all the household had risen up and flown to meet Him—He WAS alone—never to have the chance to be friends again with God—to make up for his sin by always pleasing Him, all his life long—lost! . . . lost! . . .

But he was too far sunk to support the emotion, even in recollection; and now passed into a confusion of lights, half-visions, voices, that might have belonged to the world of infancy before memory, or some entirely other world.

* * * *

A little sound came from him, like breath going out of him —as if one, wandering in some border region, not dark to sense but dim of being, had bodily encountered some Thing there.

Fearchar the Poet heard the sound and glancing down in his face saw at once that the name of the thing was Death.

2

When Byars returned home two days before, having been all night at the burning, the sun was already in the sky. He strode right through the house to a stony court at the back, merely shouting some words to the old woman as he went. In the court he laid hold of a large tub and dragged it over to the pump. He seized the handle and the water spouted. He filled the tub and dragged it a little way aside and then, standing out in the cold dawn, stripped from him every stitch of clothing, throwing the garments on the ground. Then he plunged his face and head into the tub and with loud snorts and gaspings began to wash himself. Having washed himself above the waist he got into the tub and standing in it, the water running from his soaking head and beard, washed his legs and his loins, splashing the water about. A man who had been putting up his horse appeared and at a sign from Byars began to fill a number of buckets from the pump and set them in a row. The Factor stepped out of the tub and stood waiting, and the man taking up his position a pace or two behind him, picked up one bucket after another and emptied it over him, the Factor grunting each time the cold stream soused over his head, his back, his legs. " That'll dae ye! " he shouted at last, and putting down the bucket the man stepped over to the back door of the house where the old woman had appeared a moment before with a towel in her hand and was standing, with an inquisitive expression on her face, watching the dripping Byars, who was now blowing out his cheeks and slapping his hairy strength with resounding noise. The man said something, took the towel from her, pushing her inside, and brought it to the Factor who buried his head in it and began furiously drying himself. At this point another man appeared and called out something to him. The Factor's head emerged, hair on end. " What d'ye say?" he shouted, although the man was but a pace or two away. " At Glack? Right, then! "—and went on drying himself. When he had finished, he merely swung the towel round his middle and went indoors.

Dressed in fresh clothes, and combing his hair and beard, he was entirely himself again, ruddy and glowing. Along with the dust and ashes of Gleann Luachrach he seemed to have washed from him every trace of the access that had transformed him at the height of the burning, when Maighstir Sachairi encountered him: in cheek and eye he had resumed his normal look of wholesome health, and with it even more than usual of gravity and self-possession in his air. He made as hearty a meal as some haste that appeared to be on him would allow, and immediately went out again to where his horse was held waiting.

He rode alone, at an easy pace, heading southward. When he had been going not more than half an hour he found his path obstructed. A long line of the people of Gleann Luachrach was straggling slowly past at right angles to his course, moving eastwards, towards the sea. His expression showed no hint of any kind of emotion as he went slowly through them, guiding his horse: looking neither to right nor left, nor dropping his eye on any among them, but clamly and gravely attending to his road; exactly as someone at peace with circumstances might pick a course at his ease through a crowded street where he expects to meet none of his acquaintance either friend or foe. Leaving them behind, he began to follow a track running along the edge of the low hills, the plain not far away on his left extending to the sea. It was mid-morning, bright and warm, a few clouds moving slowly eastwards, the wind dropping down to a gentle breeze. Away in the west a dull blur breaking the clear line of the hills marked where the smoke still hung in a sullen cloud above Gleann Luachrach.

When he had been riding about two hours, he turned off to the right and rode a mile towards the hills, then swung south again and mounting a steep rise, came to a halt at the top.

Below lay a small plain, about a mile across, closed in by the sloping sides of hills except to the south-east, where a narrow strip ran out on to the sweep of the plain beyond. The whole roughly circular space and lower slopes moved in changing patches with the grey-white of sheep; the place was a great natural fold: and their voices rose in a ceaseless variable sound, now distant, now close at hand. Byars sat his horse and let his eyes travel over all with a look at once observant and abstracted, as if he might have been making some calculation in his mind. Some distance down the hill a man in the dress of a shepherd was standing, leaning on a crook. Byars had noticed him from the first but ignored him while he made his calculations, his eyes narrowing in the light as they slowly followed the farthest slopes. The shepherd happened to turn his head, caught sight of him and came stepping up the hill. Two dogs that had been lying at a little distance at once got up and followed a parallel course to his, trotting quietly through the heather, trailing their feathery tails. Byars advanced down the slope.

"Aye, Lapraik," he greeted in matter-of-fact tones— "Ye're here!"

The man said something in reply in the broad accents of the South. Seeing he had stopped, the dogs after first pointing inquisitive noses towards the newcomer, quietly lay down once more. The two men continued a short time in conversation, turning to look at the sheep in the plain below.

Then—"Ye'll get word, then," said Byars in a slightly louder tone, and without a gesture or any word of farewell they parted and each retraced his steps.

On returning home Byars went straight through the house to his room. Unlocking a drawer in the tier along the wall he took out some papers and carried them to the table, and drawing up a chair under him, sat down to study them. He had left the door a trifle ajar and shortly a dog pushed its way in and going quietly up to him rested its muzzle on his knee. "H'm, that's you, is't?" he said not unkindly, glancing down, and applied himself again to what he had in hand. The dog went and lay down on the deerskin rug before the hearth, taking its time till it was settled comfortably. By and by the Factor drew forward an inkstand and taking up a pen began to write, referring now and again to the papers beside his hand. The clock ticked: the pen scratched steadily across the paper. It grew quiet in the room.

But presently the dog began to exhibit signs of uneasiness. It began twitching up its ears, looking round without raising its muzzle from between its paws, showing the whites of its eyes. It got up, then with a circular motion of its body subsided again. It expelled a loud comfortable breath, made a moist sound with its mouth, and appeared to fall asleep. But a moment later its uneasiness returned. It sat up and pricked its ears, listening.

Suddenly it was on its feet barking furiously, facing into the room. The hair standing straight up in a line along its back.

Byars gave a loud exclamation of impatience and strode to the door. " Oot wi' ye! " he shouted, holding it open, and the dog dashed out and fled through the house, wildly barking. Byars closed the door, shutting out the diminishing sound, returned to the table, and was absorbed again at once.

But not for long. For now he too began from time to time to show signs of restlessness or impatience, as if while he worked some small thing in the borders of consciousness was distracting him. And shortly it broke through his absorption. He threw down the pen and half turning in his chair sat listening.

A full minute passed. Byars sat very still in the dead quiet, his head held aside.

Suddenly he leapt to his feet with such force that the chair fell over backwards. " Gode! " he said aloud in sudden recollection, striding across the room—" Lachlan! "

He already had his hand on the door when he hesitated. Putting his ear to the panel of it, he rapped with his knuckles, calling, " Lachlan! " Then more urgently, with the beginning of banter in his tone—" Lachlan, man! Are ye deid?"

" What ails the loon that he doesna answer?" he muttered, standing back a pace. He considered the door a moment, frowning. Then stepping forward turned the key twice sharply and threw the door wide.

At the yell he gave movement started up in the house. Feet sounded outside, running. A man threw open the door; and stopped in his tracks a few paces inside it, his eyes bulging out of his head, staring past the Factor's shoulder.

In the open doorway of the cupboard a drooping, sack-like object was hanging. Byars was standing in front of it like a man in a trance. For some reason he was staring at the feet, which swung half a foot above the ground.

The man behind him made a gulping noise in his throat.

" Who wass in it?" he asked in a shaking voice—for the bloated face, with the swollen tongue protruding between the teeth, was unrecognisable.

" Zachary's Lachlan," said the Factor without turning round.

The man wheeled and dashed out. But at the door collided with another running in. " Lachlan Cearbach MacMhuirich! " he cried, urgent and breathless, " 'Sgian agad? He hass went and hangt himself! "

He went and hanged himself. After the body had been taken out and order had been restored, the words returned with the force of a phrase recollected in some connection or other to the Factor's mind. He had been a trifle shaken in fact, and before returning to his interrupted work went and filled himself a full tumblerful from a bottle which he took from a low deep shelf near the fireplace. When he had swallowed in a series of gulps a full half of the neat spirit the colour flowed back to his cheeks and brow. He was standing on the deerskin before the hearth with the half-empty glass in his hand looking across the room at the fatal cupboard.

" I *thocht* he was geyan heich! " he said softly, reflectively. And a little later—" Ye damned fule, Lachlan! Ye damned fule! "

It was then that the words returned to mind—*He went and hanged himself.* In what connection were they familiar, he wondered idly. There was a faint association somewhere . . . He frowned at the floor, pursing his lips, making his beard jut out — " *He — went — and — hanged — himself?*" — then glanced up aside at the corner of the room with a speculative eye . . .

Finding he could not recall it, he gave a little shrug, dismissing it.

One of his men opened the door and looked round the edge. " It's the meenister from Strathmeeny! "

" Heh? " said the Factor, looking up—" Oh—Oh, is't? " A look of irritation crossed his face. " Gie him a creepie in the kitchen! " he said in an arrogant tone. " He can wait my pleasure."

" He says there's hurry on him."

" *Hurry!!* " — the Factor's eyes widened amazedly — " What's his hurry to me? Gie him a creepie in the kitchen and let him goam up the lum or I'm ready." As the man's head was withdrawn he shouted after him—" An' if he doesna like it he can come back the morn—tell him that! "

He strode across to the table without another look.

" Meenisters! " he snorted, arranging his papers. " As if I hadna work o' my ain! "